Love Or Lust

By

Caudy Antoine Jr.

Copyright page

ISBN 979-8-35096-577-3

Dedication

I dedicate this book to my father, Caudy Charles Antoine SR, who died from COVID. Dad, when the world gave you clay, I watched you make art and sculptures.

I dedicate this to my Mom, who, no matter what, believed in me. My children for being the best part of me, Imani and Ma'at, My Wife Shaneequa, and my friend and partner Cynthia, who from the beginning believed in my idea.

Now, most importantly, I want to thank the prison system for giving me the time to reflect and deal with myself.

To all the people who sat back and watched me try and never helped, this book is dedicated to you.

I dedicate this book to family members who felt like you were ahead of me and my life was over. Most importantly, I dedicate this book to everyone with a dream in the middle of a Nightmare in hopes that you will live before you die.

Sincerely, Caudy C. Antoine JR.

Chapter 1

Congratulations! "Oh my God, we did it!" The day was beautiful, and the sun was shining at midday this June. Everyone was all smiles and elated. The parents were honored and excited to see their children finally graduate from high school. "Wow, we did it! I'm so proud of you." Camcorders and cell phones were everywhere, recording this event. The students looked so happy that school was finally over for at least a few months because many would be traveling far from home to take on a new challenge: first-year students, fraternities, sororities, parties, and more parties.

Still, everyone is nervous about what the future holds. This senior year has been a revelation and momentous change. Still, the time that is to come is bright, and most students are at that age where they are delighted to be considered adults and looking forward to the adventure of going away and getting out of their parent's home, leaving the nest.

"Congratulations, Lindsay!" "Thank you." Lindsay smiles and replies, showing her Colgate smile. Lindsay has the type of smile that lights up a room and causes anyone she smiles at to want to smile, too. Her deep, sun-kissed chocolate complexion is radiant as the sun bounces off her face. Lindsay is cheerful to have graduated today.

Lindsay has endured so much growing up in a single-parent household, struggling with just her mother in the two-bedroom apartment. Lindsay thinks to herself, wishing her father could have been here. He would have been so proud. Seeing his baby walk across that stage. Lindsay's father was killed in a robbery. The killer was never brought to justice. So, she has heard stories from both her mother and grandmother. They say her father was a good, hardworking man who spent his term in the army for four years, married her mother, Joanne, and wanted the best for his wife and child.

Lindsay was three when her father was killed, and she can still remember the love and comfort of her father's arms. Even at 19 years old, she still looks over pictures of her father and mother's early years. They look so content and blissful together. Anyone could see the love and affection they had for one another. Sometimes, while baking with Big Mama, Lindsay would ask her grandmother questions about her father. "Baby, your father worshiped the ground your mother walked on. They were high school sweethearts. He would walk her home from school, they would talk on the phone, and your mother was the only woman your father had eyes for. He came to me and your grandfather and asked for our blessing and permission to marry your mother; I saw the determination in that young man's eyes, and well, I knew he loved your mother, but your grandfather was a little skeptical, your grandfather was rough, especially having two daughters to raise. He drilled your father, but eventually, he let his guard down and even grew to love him as a son-in-law. When you were born, your father was so joyful, and he ran from the hospital to tell us you were born.

He was sweating and out of breath. He must have run 20 miles. I will never forget it; I remember it like it was yesterday. I was pleased but concerned. I asked David to calm down. "Baby, where is Joanne?" "At the hospital, ma'am." "And you ran here?" "Yes, ma'am." "Why?" I asked, "Where is your car?" "I forgot it." That is how excited he was to have you! Pitiful thing forgot his car wishing to tell us you were born and healthy." Big Mama almost cried. Thinking back, she had known love herself. Grandpa worked hard to supply what he could, and he passed away from lung cancer. The funny thing is, he never smoked a day in his life."

"Lindsay, my top student, congratulations!" "Oh, thank you so much, Mr. Bernstein." "I know the future will be bright for you. You will accomplish remarkable things. You have always been a leader, headstrong and determined. I'm proud of you." Lindsay is grateful that her mother, Joanne, is in attendance hugging her and here to celebrate but also to hear her teacher compliment and commend her on her work ethic and achievements. That means a lot.

Her mother works hard; well, she used to work two jobs until she got sick. Lindsay 's mom is a strong Black woman, standing 5ft 4 inches, 140 pounds, with brown eyes and a curvy figure. Her eyes can speak for her, and she has always been sickly. As of the last two and half years, her health has taken a dramatic turn, with Joanne calling her symptoms "Fire in my bones." Doctors at Duke Medical are still running bloodwork and tests to find out what is wrong. Joanne is in bed, unable to move or eat, and in pain for days at a time. Just unexpectedly, Joanne says that she has had these problems since her childhood, but never this bad. When asked to describe her pain in the past, she responded," It is worse than it has ever been." "Oh, Lindsay, look at you! You did it! I am so-so proud of you. I always knew you could do it! Come here," mother and daughter Hugged, enjoying every moment of this occasion. The sky is clear blue, matching the student's cap and gown. It is not too hot; the temperature is in the mid-70s, and everyone is enjoying themselves. "Lindsay, oh my God." Here comes Lindsay's best friends, Shaniqua And Diana. Shaniqua was beautiful. She was high yellow, 5'6", 130 pounds, with long, curly natural hair and green eyes. Some people say they change colors depending on her mood. "Hey, Miss Joanne and Lindsay, come here. Let's take a picture; oh my God, we did it!" they hug and take selfies and giggle, and Shaniqua whispers, "I almost broke my nail," looking down at her French manicured white tip nails. Shaniqua has Giuseppe shoes, a Christian Soriano Dress, and Oscar De la Renta earrings. "Girl, where are the refreshments? I am parched." Yes, Shaniqua is a diva. Shaniqua has been raised and exposed to the finer things. Her parents wanted her to have the best of everything. Yet, once in high school, Shaniqua's father suggested a public school would allow her to have an opportunity to be around "common folks," as he says. Yet, Shaniqua loves hard, and although she does not always fit in, she and Lindsay are best friends. The saying is true: opposites attract. They met in ninth grade, and Shaniqua had everything the latest. Some girls tried their best to make fun of or belittle Shaniqua, calling her stuck up or "Miss Two Good." Shaniqua would not fight - she was too good for that. But she genuinely did not know why people judged her like that because everyone who really knows her realizes who she is and understands she has a heart bigger than the state of Texas and is as good as gold. So, Lindsay could not take it anymore, and when the main girl started bullying and pushing Shaniqua, Lindsay stepped in. Let's just say those girls left Shaniqua alone. And they have been inseparable ever since. They go shopping together, to other places and events, but most of the

9

time, they are never without their other friend, Diana. Diana is 5 foot 8 inches and weighs 170 pounds. She's a mocha complexion and is built like Jennifer Lopez. God really broke the mold with her, and she is hot-blooded, being that her mother is African American and her father is Spanish. She has hazel eyes and a body that has men forget their Social Security number. She is a party animal and the adventurous one out of the bunch. But it is like she's living a double life; because of all the girls in the group, she keeps a 4.0 GPA, and her parents would never expect her to do any wrong, not their little princess, but little do they know she's a firecracker.

"Lindsay, we love you," Diana says with a Spanish accent. She looks amazing for graduation; her eyes stand out with her apricot spice eyes shadow and lip gloss, and her hair is done like always. Diana is far from Rich, but her mother is a schoolteacher, and her father is in the Air Force. "Diana is an only child, just like Lindsay and Shaniqua. Many people say only children are spoiled rotten, but I would not say that. It is safe to say that they are used to all the attention. "Oh God, can you believe it? We are going to college! Let's take a picture!" They all jump up and down and take more pictures, just soaking in the moment. The parents stand around, and then everyone hears a car honking its horn loudly in the parking lot, causing everyone's attention to focus on what's going on. "Who's that?" people gather, wondering what's going on. They see a brand new 2012 Cadillac STS V in royal blue with a ribbon, driving slowly. A tall man gets out and starts yelling and waving. That's when Shaniqua sees her uncle Donald, and she looks at her mother and father and smiles until her cheeks crack. "Oh my God, Mom, Dad, it's Uncle Donald!" she exclaims. "Yes, baby, congratulations. You know how much you mean to your mother and I," he says, looking into her eyes and assuring Shaniqua of his love for her. "Now, come on, look at your new car." "Oh, my goodness, Daddy, come on, you all, please, wow!" Shaniqua squeezes Diana and Lindsay while they all walk to the parking lot, admiring the new car. "It smells so good," Shaniqua says as the butter-soft leather seats seem to wrap around her frame. Everyone is happy, even Lindsay, who wishes she still had her father, as she sees how Shaniqua and Diana interact with their fathers. "Oh my god, thanks, Uncle Donald, thank you, Mom. What do I do with my old car?"

Shaniqua's look is comical because she is sitting in a brand-new, year-to-date Cadillac worth every bit of $65,000, and she is still worried about her five-year-old Honda Accord. "Wow," her mother replies, "Sweetheart, your father and I have decided to give it to one of your cousins as his first car." "Well, everyone, it's been a pleasure," Diana's father towers over everyone with his 6 ft 4 frame. He's dressed impeccably, from his fresh-cut Sean John sunglasses to his Ermenegildo

Zegna suit, Movado watch, and Allen Edmonds oxford shoes. He kisses his wife and daughter, Diana, "I love you, princess, and you've made me so proud. As much as I want to stay, I must report to duty at 1600 hours." "I know... I know, Dad. I love you so much, and I know how far you had to travel to get here. Thank you so much, thank you," Diana says, showing her sincerity through her body language and voice. "Oh, before I forget, here's a little graduation present," he pulls out a jewelry box. Diana jumps up into her father's arms, and he spins her around. "Wait, you don't know what's in the box yet," he teases. She reaches for the box, and he pulls her close and whispers, "Open it when you get home." "OH, Dad, please, I can't wait, gosh!" He pulls away, giving her that stern military posture and look. "Young lady, promise me you won't open it until you get home." She smiles, "I promise." They kiss, and everyone wishes each other well.

Shaniqua requested Lindsay out to eat with her mother and, of course, drive them home. Her uncle Donald drove her old car because Shaniqua is not giving up her new car keys. Everyone is joyous. All the parents offer goodbyes and promise to stay in touch. The girls have one of their Triple-B meetings. Yes, they have their own codes, and Triple-B stands for {Black, Bold, and Beautiful}. "You know it's going down at the pavilion tonight," Diana says, looking around like she has a super-secret. "What? Come on, everyone is going to be there, and of course, my Boo is performing! Yes!" she says, all fired up. "Who's your boo now? Because you seem to change up so often," Lindsay says, not throwing shade but just kidding with her homegirl. "Girl, Future," all the girls say His name and get excited.

"I don't know," Lindsay says, because for one, she's not the party type, and for two, she truly doesn't have anything to wear. Shaniqua senses this and jumps in. "Oh no, you don't! I love you, Lindsay, and we are going to paint the town red tonight, riding in my new car. I have the perfect outfit for you. Please, please," They both try hard to comfort Lindsay, showing her that both adore her. "All right, I guess I'll go," Lindsay says. "Yes!" They high-fived, knowing that they had conducted a great feat. Although all the boys in high school would hit on Lindsay, she was still a virgin, a no-nonsense type of girl. She worked hard to keep her grades up and even had part-time jobs to help her mom with the bills. She was not even thinking about boys.

"Alright, girls, come on, Diana," Diana's mother calls out.

"Coming, Mom," Diana responds.

"Bye," Shaniqua says. "Call me and be ready by 8 PM."

"Bye, Mom and Dad. I'll be home later. I'm taking Lindsay and her mom with me," Shaniqua tells her parents.

"OK, sweetheart. We love you and will be at home," they both assured her.

Lindsay helps her mother into the back seat and sits in the front while Shaniqua drives. They all laugh and joke as they head to their favorite restaurant. The year is 2012 and all three young women are proud to be part of the Class of 2012. Their world is North Carolina, with a population of 9 million (about half the population of New York) and 53,819 square miles (about twice the area of South Carolina). It is situated south of Virginia and east of Tennessee, with sub-tropical weather in the southeast of the state and a more continental climate in the mountain region. The Southern Appalachian Mountains have the Blue Ridge and Great Smoky Mountains.

Either by coincidence or fate, each young woman was born in North Carolina, in Raleigh to be exact. North Carolina is a manufacturing and agricultural state, where people grow soybeans, corn, and tobacco. It's a place where one can set up one's roots, call home, and raise a family. People here have grit, as reflected in the state motto "Esse Quam Videri," which means (To be rather than to seem)

People travel from all over the world to see what North Carolina has to offer, such as the Great Smoky Mountains National Park or Biltmore House and Gardens. This is also one of the states with the best educational and sports programs, such as Duke University and their rival North Carolina University, NC State, and Wake Forest. Many famous people who have changed the world have come from North Carolina, including Shirley Caesar, John Coltrane, Dale Earnhardt Sr., John Edwards, and Billy Graham. Yes, North Carolina has touched millions of people.

In one way or another, but right now the girls Shaniqua, Diana, and Lindsay are looking forward to what life has to offer beyond North Carolina. "Lindsay, you know Barack Obama became the first sitting president to endorse same-sex marriage today," Shaniqua brings up a topic of discussion. "I heard. I think people should be happy if that's what they want," Lindsay responds. "I guess you're right, but what about the children? Should they be exposed to what adults choose to do?" Shaniqua questions. "I don't know. That's a good question. But girl, tell me, how do I look?" Lindsay is self-conscious, like all women, but maybe more so. She is killing it dressed in a Salvatore Ferragamo dress and Christian Louboutin pumps, that Shaniqua gave her to wear as a graduation gift" Girl how do you look?" "You look amazing, wow! I couldn't even have worn that dress like you. It was made for you," Shaniqua said, seeing the smile on Lindsay's face and feeling good about making her best friend happy. Lindsay posed in front of the full-length mirror in Shaniqua's huge bedroom, which was still filled with knickknacks, stuffed animals, cheerleading trophies, and childhood photos.

"I'm so anxious to be going away to law school. Going to the Big Apple, yeah boyyyeeee," Shaniqua joked, doing a funny imitation of the Rapper Flavor Flav. Having graduated top of her class, she was accepted to NYU to study criminal law. She wants to become a defense attorney, and with the financial backing and support from her parents, her goals are achievable and realistic. At 19 years old, she plans to have her bachelor's degree by 24 and her master's degree by 28. She's figured out to make partner at a prestigious law firm, "I'm proud of you Shaniqua, you work so hard to keep your grades above average, oh I'm going to miss you so much" Lindsay says hugging her friend trying not to mess up her makeup. "Now you know you can come and visit me, and we will talk all the time it's just New York, not China you know BBB FOREVER," Shaniqua says and they Giggle and lock their pinkies as they always do.

Shaniqua's phone rings and she looks at the number, seeing its Diana. "Hey, oh my God...come downstairs right now," Diana yells into the phone. "Girl! We're on our way to pick you up! What's up? What's going on, and why are you screaming?" Shaniqua holds the phone away from her ear and looks at Lindsay, showing her confusion. "Girl, you and Lindsay come downstairs, please. I have a surprise for you." "You're over here. How did you get here? Come inside. You know I have to get myself together, and I'm not even ready yet." "Shaniqua, stop stalling. I'm out front," Diana says with a few other Spanish words that no one can understand before she hangs up. "Girl, she sounds so excited. She's downstairs. Come on, let's see what she wants," Lindsay says.

Shaniqua lives in a 10,400-square-foot home, and she has a walk-in closet just for her shoes. Her house is immaculate, and with both her parents being in the medical field, they are well off. The two-story brick home is in a gated community on Raleigh's north side. When the girls go downstairs and open the door, they are both in shock to see Diana holding a Jimmy Choo crystal and metal clutch, dressed in a red silk crepe Ramona Keveza with Jimmy Choo shoes but leaning on a black-on-black Audi RS 7 gleaming from its wash and wax. "Oh my God, wow, this is so hot!" Shaniqua complements her. They laugh and hug, and Lindsay is in awe. "Nice wheels!" "Hey, remember the jewelry box my dad gave me? Well, when I got home, this car was in our driveway, so I thought that someone was waiting on my mom, and no one was in the car, so I'm like, what the heck, right? But my mom's eyes told another story. So, I jumped out, and 'I Que Lindo!'" "Yeah, there she goes with the Spanish mess when she gets hyped." Everyone laughs. "I know, I know, I can't help it. So, I open the car, smell the seats, and grip the steering wheel, but still, I'm like, 'Mom, call Dad, please, because I want to drive it,' and she's like, 'Open your present.' And I'm like, 'Duh!' Right, and inside was a key." "WOW!" Diana was so glad. She loves her father. They all share a group hug, and Shaniqua and Diana realize that Lindsay still doesn't have a car or her father. So, to cheer her up, she at once tones the story down and compliments her dress and how she looks so beautiful. Lindsay loves Diana and is not salty or hates her. She knows Diana is content and elated about her car, and Diana hugs her friend and whispers, "Now we can drive everywhere. I love you, Lindsay. This is our car, OK?" They look at each other and lock their pinkies. "Now, what's popping? These boys have been blowing up my phone." "Oh boy," that's the other side of Diana coming out. She's popping her neck and talking smack. She's a wild girl, a firecracker, and unruly, ready to party at 20 years old and the oldest. She's also the most experienced. We can't call her a tramp, but...

CHAPTER 2

We will say she's very promiscuous. "Girl, you all remember Courtney, the tall, brown-skinned boy who plays basketball for our school? Bingo, he and Tyler, and Suave a.k.a Trey are tagging along with us. They've been blowing up my phone all day, thinking I'm playing games. Now, Suave keeps checking for you, Lindsay," Diana says with much emphasis.

"Me for what?" Lindsay is serious and nervous because she doesn't have the slightest clue what Trey aka Suave wants with her. "Why is he so anxious to see me? I've never even spoken to him. He wasn't in any of my classes. He must've bumped his head or something. I don't know him."

"See Shaniqua, here it is. Lindsay has the hottest boy in the school checking for her, and she doesn't even have a clue. Girl, get with the program. You are so out of the loop. He's hot like gasoline being poured on a forest fire. Girl, please work with me. And Tyler is with you, Shaniqua. Tyler was a jock, a big-time quarterback for the high school. Rumors are all the D1 schools want him for leading Southeast High School to the third championship."

"Oh, he's cute, but I don't know. I just thought it was a girl's night out."

"It is, but you two old ladies need to loosen up, please. Plus, they're paying for us. It's Sauvé's treat."

"His treat? That's $60. Where does he work?" Lindsay asks, still concerned with these boys' intentions.

"Don't know, don't care tonight. I get to see my baby for free, and I can see if Courtney is packing."

"Oh, gross. Way too much info," Lindsay says, and Shaniqua just stands there with her mouth wide open.

"You are so ratchet." They all laugh and go back inside to get dressed.

Southeast Valley High School was the school that the girls attended. So did Courtney, Tyler, and Tre aka Suave. While Courtney was a ball player and although he wasn't D1 material, he had the potential to be someone on the ball court. Suave was in the streets heavy, but somehow, he managed to walk across the stage and get his diploma. But he was known by everyone to come from a family of pimps and hustlers. He would often hang out at Club Divas on Newbern Avenue in Raleigh, and his uncle Cisco had a pool hall on the boulevard. He didn't have any plans to go to college; he was too busy chasing panties and paper.

"What's good, fool?" he says, giving a handshake to his homeboys Courtney and Tyler.

"Shoot, you know, ready to mingle," Courtney says, brushing his waves and smiling from ear to ear, shaking hands with Tyler.

All the young men were dressed up. Courtney was in Polo from head to toe, from his shirt with the big horse to his chinos and Polo boots with the buckles. Tyler was wearing True Religions and a pair of forces, while Suave was wearing APC jeans and a white shirt by Giorgio Armani, with his platinum chain and Virgin Mary piece hanging, and his 2-carat diamond earrings in both his ears. And, on his feet, he had on a pair of Jordan Fives.

"Yō, y'all ready to go all the way, because it's going down tonight."

"Here, pop one of these," Suave pulls out some pills inside of a Mentos container and passes it around.

"What's this, candy? Mints?"

"Yeah, candy, now take one" Suave said. Courtney nervously takes a pill, not wanting to seem lame or disappoint Suave, who is so cool. he puts it in his mouth and swallows it dry before passing the rest to Tyler. "No man, I'm good. Those look like X pills. I'm straight. My brothers told me that stuff has all kinds of drugs in it, like heroin and cocaine. Nah, that isn't for me. I'm headed to the pros," he says, clapping his hands and holding his head up, smiling, and confident. "That's what's up. I hear you, boy, and you better hold a brother down with some tickets when you play for the Carolina Panthers," Suave says as they both bump fists.

Courtney feels embarrassed but tries to play it off. He's never taken drugs before tonight and just found out that he took a pill with different substances. He's feeling low. Suave lights up some loud (weed), takes a few pulls, and both Courtney and Tyler pass on smoking. After listening to Suave talk with some chick on the phone, they ride out to meet the girls.

When they pull up to the pavilion, it's packed in the parking lot. It's like a car show with pimped-out Dunks, Chevys, and Cadillacs, but Suave is crushing the game. He pulls up in a silver-waxed 2002 Bentley Continental GT on 28-inch rims. It's an old model, but he's only 19 years old and doesn't have a job. All the girls are in awe, and he calls out to some from the driver's side window, "Yeah, baby, what's shaking? Oh yeah, what's good?" He's feeling himself big-time and finally after circling the parking lot parks and finds the girls, when they link up all the girls are flawless, and everyone greets one another.

Suave approaches Lindsay like he's God's gift to women. "What's good, boo?" he says, grabbing onto her. But before she can answer, Lindsay shuts him down. "Stop, please don't touch me," she says firmly. Suave sees how serious she is and falls back. Lindsay can't stand anyone touching her, let alone someone she doesn't know, and she can also smell the smoke and cigarettes on him. "Yuck."

Suave plays it off and compliments Diana on her car. "Man, I'm thirsty," Courtney says as the ecstasy pill starts to take effect. Now he's feeling groovy. Cars in the parking lot are blasting music, and the guys escort the ladies toward the entrance. Suave stays close to Lindsay like he's claiming her, and everyone gives him head nods and attention. Because If they're an item, Lindsay is a catch, but if you pay very close attention, Lindsay isn't even thinking about Suave or his sorry advances.

"The line is back here. Where are we going, cutting all these people?" Shaniqua asks with concern.

"Chill, little mama. I got this. Trust me," Suave says, going to the front of the line. "Yō, hold up! Oh, what's good Suave What's Poppin', bro? You tell your uncle Cisco what I said?" the big black security guard asks Suave after shaking his hand and hugging him. Suave and the security guard converse first, and then Suave shows off by pulling out a wad of money and slowly peeling off six $100 bills. Still holding up the line, he hands them to the security guard, who then ushers everyone into the building.

Suave tries to put his arm around Lindsay, but she brushes him off. He looks around, thrown into a state of self-consciousness. Little does anyone know, the security guard is in debt to Sauvé's uncle, so he's not even charging them to get in, and its half-price for everyone with Suave. The rest of the money Suave will get back later, but he feels the need to be seen and show off.

As soon as they get into the party, the music artist Future is performing his hit song "Hey There, Hey There." The ladies are going crazy, screaming his name, followed by the song. "My fingers, they are itching for the paper."

"Wow, that was impressive," Diana says while taking a few more pulls of the marijuana joint that Suave passed her. Lindsay and Shanique refuse to smoke! period. Courtney is smiling and waving at everyone and rubbing on himself while leaning on Sauvé's Bentley. "Man, this car is so hot, man," he says. Now he's walking around the car and rubbing on it. Tyler sees he's making a fool of himself, and grabs hold of him. "Wow, player, get a hold of yourself man, you're tripping the ladies out," he whispers, smiling to everyone. Suave, on the other hand, is bent over laughing. He knows that Courtney is on ecstasy and he's high as a kite right now, and he's laughing at him. Shaniqua is concerned for Courtney. She's never seen him act like this. Courtney tries to hug Tyler. "I love you, man, seriously, I love all, of you guys. I love all human beings." "Oh, that stuff is really kicking in now. That's a triple stack," Suave says, clapping his hands together and laughing. "Shaniqua, come on, I'm ready to go," Lindsay says. She looks around the parking lot. Most people are headed to the waffle house or any after-party spots to continue to party, but Lindsay refuses to be a part of the club scene.

A car pulls up, and Suave starts talking loud to the female driving the car. "Yeah, baby, you know me, Mackin', and keeping it 100 out here. So, what's good? Why haven't I heard from you?" Suave leans in the driver-side window, talking into the girl's ear. Lindsay sees the girl make eye contact with her as if Suave has said something about her, and the girl driving the car rolls her eyes. Lindsay is confused but by no means going to let this girl think she's afraid of her, so she rolls her eyes back. "Suave, who is that bitch?" "Who are you calling a bitch? You don't even know me," Lindsay replies. "Suave says you're just a jump off anyway," the girl says, as Suave looks like he just bit into a lemon. Now Lindsay is pissed all the way off. "His jump off? I don't even know him, and I'm not here with him, so get your story straight."

"Whatever, then why did he pay your way in? OK, oh cat gotcha tongue?" Lindsay was hot.

"Shaniqua, let's go please," Lindsay said, walking away. She could hear Suave say, "Let that stuck-up bitch go." He had tried desperately to win her over by flashing money and buying drinks, but truthfully, Lindsay was different. Diana and Shaniqua were straightening Suave.

"Listen, don't talk about her like that, she doesn't deserve that." "Yes, Suave, that's not cool." "Whatever." Shaniqua and Diana caught up with Lindsay. She is so upset she has tears in her eyes. Tyler and Courtney are stuck in between, so Suave speaks.

"You rolling or what? because we're headed to the Waffle House?" Courtney is grinning from ear to ear. "I'm hungry, I'm going with you." Courtney looks pitiful, trying to hug Suave. "Courtney, man, get off me, man, you clown, go get in the car!" he yells, embarrassing him.

Tyler looks on and decides to catch up to the girls. "Suave, thanks, but no thanks, I'll get with you." "Yeah, whatever," Suave says, throwing shade. Tyler catches up to the girls as Diana is removing her shoes to start driving back to Shaniqua's house.

"Diana, wait, listen. Suave was out of pocket, and believe me, I didn't have anything to do with that. Please don't hold me accountable for his childish actions, and Lindsay," he says, looking into the car, "I know you probably don't want to hear this, but he's a jerk, and don't let his insecurities determine your night. Look, we've graduated, and he's mad because he can't manipulate you into thinking he is more than what he is, so please know I had nothing to do with that."

Although Lindsay is to hurt to talk, she looks into his eyes and sees his sincerity, and nods her approval. "Tyler, how are you getting home? I see that jerk driving by with Courtney, waving out the window like a two-year-old." Suave drove by while Tyler was consoling Lindsay. "I'm going to call my brother." "Wait, I'll take you home." Tyler accepts the offer and gets into the car. First, they ride and drop Lindsay off at the Kingwood Forest Apartments, then drive north on Sandal Ford Road to Shaniqua's, and after that, Diana and Tyler are riding alone after dropping Shaniqua off and telling her to call tomorrow.

Tyler breaks the silence by explaining how Courtneys behavior was uncalled for and truthfully, "He should have been proud to be on a date with a girl like you, because any guy in his right mind would have cherished that opportunity."

"Thanks, Tyler, I didn't know you were so mature. I mean I've seen you around school and yes, I realize you're a star quarterback, but tonight I'm able to see another side of you," Diana says while looking over to the passenger seat into Tyler's brown eyes.

"So, how long have you and Courtney been kicking it?" Tyler asks. Diana gives him a sour look and he speaks, "You're right, let's not even talk about him anymore." They both smile.

Now Diana is still feeling a buzz and, although Tyler was supposed to hook up with Shaniqua, from talking to Tyler and seeing the distance between the two after dropping Shaniqua off, Diana has a notion that Tyler and she may have some chemistry.

"So, tell me, where do you see yourself in the next four years?" Diana laughs before answering his question. "What's so funny?" he says, smiling, blown away by Diana's beauty.

"Well, I don't know about the next four years, but I'm sure about the next hour," she says while reaching over and gently squeezing his leg. "Oh gosh," Tyler tries to play it cool, but her words, her touch, all of it is too much, and he almost jumps out of his seat. Now, Tyler knows his way around the football field, but he's always been a gentleman when it comes to the ladies. Yes, he doesn't have much experience. He's not a virgin mentally because he's watched porn, but he's never gone all the way, so yes, technically, he's a virgin. "Where are we going?" Tyler asks as the sound of the music artist JOE comes through the speakers. "I can read your mind, baby. I know what you're thinking". "Chill somewhere special." Diana takes Tyler to Wilmington, and together they walk the beach and lay on a blanket. The sky is beautiful, the sand is warm in between their toes, and after talking and vibing, Tyler agrees to give Diana a back massage. While rubbing her shoulders, she sees he's nervous and guides him, coaches him, and tells him to remove the top of her dress and bra. Tyler is now hard as a statue as he rubs her soft skin while she lays on her stomach on the blanket. Diana is hot and aroused now and turns onto her back, looking up at Tyler, seeing his innocence and loving the power she has over him. She can feel his energy, his raw masculinity. "Come here, kiss me," Tyler is impressed by her pleasing breasts, and he kisses her gently until inexperience gives way and instinct takes over, and passion surfaces. Now, his lips and tongue are all over her breasts and nipples, her areolas. She's completely engrossed and out of her dress, nude, riding him. The feeling for both is magnificent.

"Oh yes, deep, so deep," Diana can feel Tyler on her G spot, bringing her to multiple orgasms. And when Tyler finally feels that build-up from his spine to his groin and he explodes, it is the greatest feeling in the world. "Oh God, yes, oh!" To Tyler, this is special, and he tries to hold Diana, but she kills that notion. "Oh wait, I feel sticky, let's go."

Diana becomes distant as she always does. Tyler is confused. In his mind, they just shared something exceptional or rare, but to Diana, he was just another conquest. Diane is not worried that Tyler didn't pull out because she is on birth control and the Depo shot.

After dropping Tyler off, she took his number but refused to give him hers. Tyler, although he lost his virginity, he's learned a valuable lesson. Women also just have sex at times with no feelings involved.

As soon as Lindsay got home, she was so upset about her night with that idiot Suave or whatever his name was because that's how she felt. She just wanted to forget his whole existence, so without deviation, she got into the shower and was going to crawl into bed. But something told her it was too quiet, and to check on her mother, so she did.

And when bending down to kiss her forehead after entering her mother's room and turning off the flat-screen TV. "Mama, hey, I told you, you always fall asleep watching that TV and the TV ends up watching you," Lindsay says in a faint voice while picking up and straightening things out around her mother's bedroom when she realizes how warm her mother's skin felt. So, she goes and rubs her head again.

"My God, you're hot," Lindsay says as she rubs her chest. Lindsay now sees that her mother is running a fever, and her breathing is strained and shallow. "Oh, mama, wake up, please talk to me." She was not getting a response, so she called 911.

"911, what's your emergency?" Lindsay tries to remain calm and tell the operator exactly what the problem is. After hanging up, she gently dabs a cold washcloth on her mother's head and chest until the paramedics arrive.

A few hours later, Lindsay is seen talking to the doctor. The hospital is quiet and serene at this hour, and the doctor seems concerned and extremely helpful in explaining Lindsay's mother's condition. "Your mother Joanne was running a severe fever, and she was having serious respiratory problems. We plan to keep her overnight just to run some more tests and find out more about the health and state of your mother."

"Thank you, Dr. Clark. She's been sick for a while now, but I don't know, it just seems to be getting worse," Lindsay says while a single tear rolls down her beautiful face.

"Here now, don't cry. We will run some tests and do some bloodwork and try to find out what's wrong". "Yes, Dr. Clark, thank you. She's all I have. I don't want to lose her; I don't know what I would do without her," Lindsay says.

"Don't stress yourself. Everything will work out. Let go and let God, young lady. Trust me! Now, here's my number. Call if you have any questions. Now, please go home, get some rest, and you can pick up your mother 24 hours from now. OK, now relax, breathe, and take this slow. She's well cared for," Dr. Clark smiles and assures her that her mother will be safe.

Lindsay calls her grandmother to explain that she was at the hospital and that her mother was OK, and she took a cab back to Kingwood Forest Apartments. Lindsay looks around at her apartment complex and sees a few older and young Black men standing around early in the morning, talking and texting on cell phones, cars pulling up, and fiends and addicts roaming to and from. She plans to get her mother out of this place. This environment isn't healthy for anyone. She just needs a plan.

She walks into the house after paying the cab driver and crawls into bed. A few hours later, her phone kept ringing. "Ring, ring, ring."

"Hello."

"Wake up, sleepyhead."

"Yeah, get up, lazy. Hey, rise and shine."

"What time is it?" Lindsay asks after hearing both Shaniqua and Diana's voices on the phone. They both answer at the same time. "3:30 in the afternoon, girl. What have you been doing?" Diana asks.

CHAPTER 3

With a sneaky voice. "Girl please, I've been at the hospital all morning." Lindsay replies. The girls listened carefully and after listening to Lindsay explain about her mother's situation, they offered their support and sympathy. "Oh, I love Miss Jones. I'm going with you to pick her up," Shaniqua says, not taking no for an answer. Then the conversation leads to what everyone will do and what school they have chosen to attend this fall. Diana has chosen UCLA to study bioengineering and plans to leave in two weeks. Her mother and father are both in agreement and in support of her move, even though the school is on the West Coast. "I think it would be good for you to travel and see the other side of the country, get out of Raleigh."

"Oh yeah, don't forget to meet new boys with your freaky self," Shaniqua says, and they all laugh. "I'm not freaky, I just like to have fun."

"Yeah right, you having fun is like Pinky and Cherokee on film."

"What? How do you know Cherokee, is my role Model?" They all crack jokes and clown around.

"So, Shaniqua, have you figured out where you're going?"

"Yes, I'm sure now. I'm going to the Big Apple to study law at NYU. I'll leave next month, and I'm so nervous."

"Oh, I'm so proud of you. What kind of law do you plan to study?"

"Criminal. I want to try to help. I believe a lot of people need a good lawyer in their corner, and someday I want to make partner in a good firm. That's where the real bucks are," she adds with a smile.

"Oh boy, then you'll really have your own shoe store just for your shoes," Lindsay says.

"How did you know?"

"Please give me discounts on Giuseppe's, please, pretty please," Diana begs.

"What about you, Lindsay?"

"Yes, Lindsay, I forgot you had so many offers with running track and your GPA. Girl, you could go anywhere. Right now, I'm jealous."

"Well, right now Colgate University in Hamilton, New York, offered me a full scholarship academically, and a couple of other Ivy League schools."

"Colgate, girl, that's like $50,000 a semester. Dang."

"Also, Fayetteville State for the track team and NC State, but with Mom's condition, I'm not sure where I'm going because I can't see myself just up and leaving her when she needs me right now."

"Oh wow, I feel you. I wish there was something I could do to help." Both Diana and Shaniqua agree. Lindsay knows that her mother wants the best for her, but with her physical condition, she is 100% willing to sacrifice to help her mom through this terrible time.

A week later, Diana and Shaniqua both decide to go shopping together. "Girl, you know Samsung has a new phone that's water-resistant?" Diana says excitedly.

"Wow, I need one of those. It just makes sense. If you drop your phone in the sink or get it wet, you don't have to worry anymore." Diana replied,

"Shaniqua Isn't it crazy how the police keep shooting all these Black men lately? If they keep it up, there won't be any Black men left."

Diana commented "Yeah, I've seen the footage on the news, and it's really sad because a lot of the men had their hands up. That's one of the reasons why I want to study law, to help make a difference and show that not just Black lives matter but all lives matter."

Shaniqua Said "You got that right, damn girl. Look at him, "

Diana yelled "There you go, Diana? You can't go one day without flirting." (They both laugh)

"I'm Latino, what do you expect?" Diana said snapping her neck. (Smiling).

Shaniqua parks the car and together they walk to the mall. It's partly sunny and breezy today. A thunderstorm in the southern mountains will clear too partly cloudy tonight. The ladies were enjoying the day.

"Girl, I just love this Olay brightening cream cleanser." Shaniqua smells it and thinks of purchasing it when She remembers that she already has three at home.

"It's weird having to shop for clothes for the winter. I've never been, but I hear it gets cold in New York." Shaniqua states.

"That's crazy, right? And I must shop for things to show my butt off in."(They laugh)

"Girl, you're a mess. So, whatever happened to that guy Tyler? Sometimes I think maybe I should have given him my number. I mean, he was nice, had a pleasant easy-going nature."

"Yes, but his thing was little." Diana just flat out said.

"What? Hell no, you didn't." Shaniqua said with a big smile. Diana tickled her saying "Yes, I did."

"I don't believe it. Get out of here, When? that night?" Shaniqua asked "Yes, while you were rubbing your clit, I was enjoying his company. Diana said. With a grin. "I don't do that, thank you." Replied Shaniqua

"Well, you should. We had sex on the beach in Wilmington. He can kiss, but his meat is little."

"My God, you are full of surprises."

"Are you mad? Shaniqua, please don't let him ruin our friendship."

"Mad? No, no, I don't even know him. You hooked or tried to hook us up with ghetto-wannabe Suave or whatever his name is, and I had no idea Courtney was a loser. No, I'm cool. I wish you had told me."

"I'm sorry. He wasn't worth talking about, that's all. BBB."

"Always." The ladies join pinkies and keep shopping. Shaniqua spent over $15,000 with a credit card, and the trunk of the car was full of designers like Marc Jacobs, Jimmy Choo pumps, Bally turtlenecks, Marion Ayonote shoes, Tom Ford boots, Dolce Gabbana, you name it, and Shaniqua bought it. Diana splurges, but only worth $7,000 because there are only so many bikinis and shorts one can have. But she did go crazy at the sneaker store and bought Jordans. She also bought a sleek timepiece by Michael Kors - a rose gold-toned watch for $250 to match her Jordans.

After tearing down the mall, the girls went to Lindsay's of course, To take her something and eat together, as they always do. The only reason Lindsay didn't go shopping was that she was still working a part-time job. She couldn't make it, but they didn't forget their best friend. They both bought gifts for her to show their love. When they arrived, Lindsay still wasn't home, but Miss Jones was. The aroma from the kitchen knocked them off their feet. It smelled so good. "Oh, hi, girls. What a surprise! Come in, oh, please come in praise God."

"Hey Miss Joanne, how are you?" they both asked, embracing the frail body of Joanne, and feeling her discomfort as they hugged her. Shaniqua looked into Miss Joanne's eyes and saw that although her body was weak, her spirit was strong. The young women looked around and the house was clean as always. Judging from the inside, you would guess that they were living somewhere in the suburbs, but looking from the outside, it was far from where Shaniqua and Diana were raised - in Kingwood Forest Apartments. Still, the young women felt safe and comfortable with Miss Joanne and Lindsay.

"Where is Lindsay? She was supposed to be off already, and she's not answering the phone," Shaniqua asked in a concerned tone, while Diana was on her phone texting some guy, she met a few days ago. It was hard to hear Joanne, so Shaniqua left Diana on the couch and went into the kitchen.

"She'll be here later, sweetie. The boss needed her to stay over because someone was sick, and the Lord knows we need the money, but I wish my health was a lot better. I had to let one of my jobs go, and the doctor still doesn't know what is wrong with me. I go to church, I pray, and I try to do right by people, but sometimes I swear," Miss Joanne said. Fatigue was written on her face as she moved pots around in the kitchen.

Shaniqua hugged Joanne again to reassure her that things would be okay. "That's so kind of you," Miss Jones said. "Lindsay works so hard I plan to cook this meal for her. Lord knows she deserves it."

"It smells so good," Diana says, popping into the kitchen and smiling from ear to ear. Joanne and Shaniqua share a smile. "What are you making?"

"Skillet roasted chicken, Lindsay's favorite. I took a 5-pound chicken, kosher salt and freshly ground black pepper, sprigs, fresh thyme and rosemary, garlic smashed and peeled and cut into little cubes like this, carrots, parsnip, sweet potatoes, the works," Joanne shows them and the young women's mouths begin to water. "And also 3 tablespoons of olive oil."

"Mom, I'm home," Lindsay was tired. She had ridden the bus from work and smiled wide and bright when she saw both Shaniqua and Diana. Lindsay hugged the girls hard and Lindsay kissed her mother before washing up to prepare to help.

"Wow, it smells good. Oh, Mama, you didn't have to go through all this trouble."

"Girl, hush. You're my baby. I love you and don't think that I don't know how hard you've been working. And leaving money in my purse. Lindsay, you're grown now, and your father would be so proud to see how you've become a mature, independent young woman. It's time for you to move on, no listen, baby." Joanne says in almost a whisper, never the one to raise a voice. "This place needs to be put behind you. You're smart and athletic, the world is your oyster. You must open it up and I know that my health hasn't been the best. Sometimes I can't handle getting out of bed. I'm in so much pain. But, Angel, I refuse to make you suffer and miss out on your blessings because of me."

All the women are listening, sitting at the table with tears in their eyes because it's the truth that Lindsay has so much potential.

"Mama, I can't leave you like this."

" You must, baby. Love Don't hold nobody love, Let's go. I know you better than you know yourself. I've bathed you in the sink and changed your stinking Pampa," Miss Joanne says, softly smiling and squeezing her daughter's delicate hand. "Now, promise me that you'll follow your dreams because I'm proud of you, Lindsay, and you will do great things. Oh no, just promise me."

"I promise, mama." "All right, let me say grace so we can eat." The women listened to music while eating and time seemed to fly bye. Miss Joanne fell asleep, and the girls helped straighten up the kitchen. Lindsay loved the clothes she got from her best friends and eventually Shaniqua and Diana left to head home.

Two weeks later, Lindsay spoke to Shaniqua, "Can you believe I'm leaving for New York tomorrow? Gosh, time flew by." "Yes, you're going to be a Yankee in no time. What's up, son?" Lindsay laughed as she and Shaniqua talked on the phone. "I'm so nervous. I'm going to call you all the time. You deal with people better than I do. I'm going to need your advice." "About what?" "Everything, girl. You know I've been here all my life." "Just be yourself and be cautious. Everyone will not have your back or best interest at heart, but overall, Shaniqua, you'll be fine." "I guess you're right. God, I'm going to miss you."

"Hey, Lindsay, does having sex on the first date equal a permanent booty call?" "What the heck are you talking about? Have you been on those websites again?" "No, I mean, yes, but under a different name. You know I'm still a virgin, girl? And I want to wait." "I know, I know, for Prince Charming." "Really, seriously. So, I'm just curious," "Shaniqua were both virgins and you already know how I feel about sex. It has to be real, well, Thought out. Men think if a woman lets him get her goods on the first night, most men will look at her like a jump-off," "I guess, but it also depends on how she carries herself later. If she presents herself as a sex toy, then yes." "Are you considering a one-night stand?"

"No, Lindsay. It was just a topic of discussion."

"Well, sex is the furthest thing from my mind. I've chosen to attend FSU." Lindsay replied.

"Florida State? Wow."

"No, Fayetteville State. You know I can't go too far from Mama. That way, I would not be but a couple of hours from her. She's sick, and she's all I have. I would never forgive myself if I let something happen to her."

"That's what I love about you, Lindsay. You always try to help others. You have a big heart, and God will always protect you."

"Thank you. I love you too. And call me when you get to New York." "I Will That's Diane on the other line. OK, good-bye."

One year later

"Lindsay wait up" "You need to hurry" "I'm coming Dang!!!" "I'm just ready to get packed and head home to see my mother and grandmother" Lindsay said. "I understand I'm going back to Tennessee to visit my sister is excited for me to finally meet my new nephew, did I show you his picture Lindsay?" "Yes only 100 times" Lindsay said smiling "I know Lindsay but he's so cute." "He is adorable"

Lindsay was collaborating with her roommate, Natasha. Natasha started as a first-year student like Lindsay, and they'd been studying and living together in the dorm for a year now. Natasha is a long-distance runner for the women's track team.

She's from Jackson, Tennessee, slim, pretty, with a strong southern accent. She holds records in the 3000 Meter Steeplechase and has the potential to be great. Lindsay and Natasha have become friends over time. Lindsay enjoys their company and friendship, although they're not as close as she is to Shaniqua and Diana. Natasha's body is amazing. She's a vegan and very conscious about her health. She works hard at whatever she does and is aiming to eventually qualify for the Olympics. The only problem that Lindsay has is that some weekends, Natasha's boyfriend sneaks into the dorm room, and let's just say that the sounds of their lovemaking are becoming too much for Lindsay. Her sexual frustration is starting to take a toll. She thought about masturbating, but she's confused and uncomfortable about it, and sometimes she acts like she's asleep when Derek and Natasha are going at it. She can feel her vaginal walls clench just thinking about Derek pumping away at Natasha. A lot of men have tried to woo Lindsay, but she still just focuses on her studies.

"Girl, what is wrong, Lindsay? Talk to me. You've been crabby lately, and you're my girl. What's up?" Natasha asks, trying to find the underlying cause of it.

"Nothing," Lindsay says while packing a suitcase. Spring break is approaching, and some students are going on vacation or going home, while others plan to just stay on campus and relax.

"Lindsay, come on. We've been together for almost a year. Give me some credit, girl. I know it's not that time of the month because we normally have our friend pay us a visit around the same time," Natasha says, smiling trying to make light of the situation. Natasha walks over to Lindsay and gently embraces her. "You know I'm here if you need me."

"I know, Natasha. I'm all right. Just a little worried about my family," Lindsay says. That was the truth, but her hormones were going haywire, and she couldn't explain it. "And by the way, that was a great run."

"Thanks," Natasha responds, happy to see Lindsay smile.

Lindsay had run the 200 m (about 656.17 ft) semifinal heat in 19.74 seconds, coming in first. What made it so spectacular was that it was raining. Lindsay led her school to another victory.

In the morning, Lindsay got a ride from a girl on the track team to the Trailways bus station. After getting a ticket, she only had to wait 15 minutes for her bus's departure to Raleigh. Lindsay boarded the bus and put her overhead luggage away. She got comfortable in her window seat and put her iPod into her ears to listen to Alicia Keys' album and relaxed. Lindsay needed to stretch her legs.

She thought about using the bathroom, but she figured she would wait until she got home. Using the bathroom on the bus or at the bus station was gross, and just the thought made her feel uncomfortable.

When she got off the bus at Moore Square station, she felt good and felt that home had not changed much. It had been a Year and she was returning from college life. Downtown, she took the number five bus, which went from downtown to her apartment complex. Riding the bus was always a hassle, and she couldn't wait to get herself a car.

While riding the bus, she sat by the window, and after several stops of people getting on and off the bus, Lindsay paid close attention to the prison. The prison looked different. She could still remember when she was a little girl, and her mother Joanne would ride by the prison.

"Mommy, mommy, what's that big building?"

"Oh, don't you worry about that? That place is for bad people." Now, for some strange reason, she felt a connection to the place, just a feeling that it was more visible now. Lindsay reached her stop and saw a few familiar faces and spoke to friends or associates rather.

"Hi."

"Hey, Lindsay. We missed you," Joanne was waiting at the front door with a great big smile along with Big Mama. They all hugged, and it felt warm all over they were happy to be in each other's company again.

Chapter 4

"What's this do? I mean how is it going to make me feel?" Diana asked as she sat in the passenger seat of the candy-apple red Porsche Boxster GTS convertible.

"Like a star, just sit it on your tongue, and here, drink this orange juice," Todd replied as he started the car and crawled around Los Angeles. Diana was dressed in only a bikini, and her curves and breasts were getting major attention from other drivers.

Todd and Diana were returning from the beach and headed to his loft downtown. Todd was an IT Internet technician, and his parents were very wealthy. Diana met him shortly after joining the sorority at her school, Delta PHI Zeta. Diana made it through all the hazing and humiliating obstacles, and now she's a full-fledged member. This first year has been a blur for her; Party after party, she even changed her major to computer programming and minor to psychology.

As the pill started to take effect, Diana felt completely different. Her pupils were dilated, and she was now laid back in the seat with the wind blowing in her face. Diana had been keeping a 75% GPA average, with a C average in school her parents were bound to ask questions. When questioned by her mom, who is a schoolteacher, Diana never accepts responsibility and blames it on the professors and her just trying to make the transition. "Mom, don't worry, I'll do better next semester."

They pulled into the garage, and Todd parked the Porsche next to his Aston Martin DB 9 vanquish. Todd was bare-chested, dressed in Nautica shorts and sandals. He squeezed Diana's breast, and she comes out of her daze. "Are we there yet?" Diana asked.

"Yes, sweetheart," Todd replied. Todd had blonde hair, ice blue eyes, and his family were of German descent, with extraordinarily strong Nautical features. Todd is almost ten years older than Diana, who is a first-year student. She has been with the older crowd since attending school and has been crashing parties since her first weekend on campus. She has plane tickets to leave for North Carolina in two days and decided to spend a day at the beach with Todd before heading out.

They took the elevator to his loft, and extravagance is not the word. Todd's interior decorator did not slouch on any of the perks, turning his loft into a bachelor's paradise. All the furniture is matching color combinations of black, white, and crimson, and every piece seems to have been imported or handcrafted. Todd has been born into wealth; his parents have recently, in the past ten years, watched one of their investments rise to a net income of 31%. They had over 75,000 shares in Paragon Bank, which successfully completed a $28.7 million Initial public offering. When the shares of the company were bought by Todd's parents at two dollars per share and eventually rose to $300, per share they made millions. On the walls. Is fine art, statues of nude mermaids and erotic sculptures, and people are moving about to the sounds of techno music gyrating and free-spirited in the nude. And, on the coffee table, there's a bowl the size of a punch bowl filled to the brim full of different colored pills, similar to the one Diana took in the car.

Not far from here, Santa Clarita wildfires drive thousands from their homes. A landscape of desiccated fuel has created explosive conditions for a fire averaging 10,000 football fields. Rescue crews and firefighters are using drones and water-dropping helicopters to put the fires out.

Yet here Inside the loft, young men and women aren't concerned or caring about the news. This is a nonstop party. The housekeepers pick up and clean when necessary. Diana is in a zone. The vibrations of the music are causing her body to move and groove. A young, skinny, surfer-tanned guy with long sandy blonde hair and nude, just like everyone else, walks up to Diana and tongue-kisses her. Their lips meet and their tongues begin to dance in one fluid motion. His long fingers are pulling her hands gently, guiding her to an area of the loft.

Diana sees women kissing women, men kissing men, and people covered in latex. She's so high, and every nerve seems to feel everything, every fiber of her being. She's led to a leather couch; hands bend over her. She feels two hands at first, caressing her, then four, hands everywhere. Her breasts, thighs, and back starting to tingle and Diana arches her back. She lets go of any insecurities and just lives in the moment. She feels her bikini come off. Now someone is pulling her hair gently and penetrating her from behind. Before she realizes it, there's another man entering her mouth. She's blown away. Now she feels someone's fingers penetrating her rectum, pushing a strange object, which she recognizes as a pill – yes, a pill – inside of her. Her orgasm was a blur, and so is the rest of the night.

New York

"Can you hold one minute, Lindsay?" Shaniqua yells

"Get the fuck out of the way!" the light is freaking green, green means Go, go bitch, I have shit to do!" Shaniqua was cursing like a sailor, weaving through traffic. Lindsay is listening; her voice can be heard over the speakers in the Cadillac she's driving. "Shaniqua, is that you?" Lindsay shouted Lindsay is shocked. She's never heard Shaniqua curse before, but city life is really changing Shaniqua. In the last year, Shaniqua has managed to keep her grades above average, and success has just been chasing Shaniqua down because of her devotion and hard work. She has been introduced to a lawyer who has his own firm named Mr. Johnson, Peter Johnson the Third. He has two brothers who make up Johnson and Johnson's law firm on the Lower East Side of Manhattan. In law, there are programs devoted to preparing individuals for the practice of law and other law-related careers here in the United States. Legal education is conducted by about 200 law schools around the country, some are units of public or private colleges and universities. There are very few law schools that are independent. Now most states vary in law. In practically all states completion of law school is required before someone may take a bar examination, and one must pass the bar examination (exam) to become a lawyer. Also, an individual may serve an apprenticeship in a law office for several years as an alternative to law school. Shaniqua has many options, her family and professors at the university feel that it would be in her best interest to continue a few classes at the school and, most importantly, take the offer of an apprenticeship with Johnson and Johnson's law firm.

"Yes, Lindsay, I'm still here. What's good, girl? I miss you sooooo... much. I'm going to be in Raleigh tonight. My flight leaves at 8 PM. I'll arrive at 9:30 PM. So, tell me, what's been going on with you, country bumpkin?" Lindsay looked at the phone and smiled. That's my Home girl, and after a year in the Big Apple, she has obviously been bitten by a sewer rat. Her accent has changed; she's louder. I mean, she's yelling like she's talking in an auditorium. Lindsay thinks to herself, "God, where do I start? The track is good, Fayetteville State is cool, my roommate, oh my gosh, she's a great runner!" "Hold up, Lindsay, I know this bitch isn't trying to act like I didn't see that parking space first. Miss, cut it out, please, cut the bullshit!" Shaniqua says, "Let me call you back, got to straighten this shit ASAP."

"OK, bye." Wow, the first thing Lindsay thinks when she gets off the phone with Shaniqua is I don't want to live in New York. Lindsay has been trying to call Diana, but her phone keeps going to voicemail. By noon, Shaniqua pulls up into Lindsay's apartment complex in her year-to-date rented black Tesla series sedan. The electric car had everything - Bluetooth, Wi-Fi, and internet. A couple of guys were standing around, tapping one another on the shoulders. "Look, man, Yo, you see that?" Shaniqua is used to attention, but she looks disgusted with these bottom feeders. Shaniqua steps out in black jean shorts that show the contour of her hips and backside. She wore a leather sleeveless vest which was black and white to match her black belt and high stilettos "Miss Jones," she greets Miss Joanne at the front door and can hear Lindsay in the back getting ready. They were going to spend the entire day together, going shopping and out to eat, but most importantly, to catch up on things. This last year is the longest they've ever been apart since high school, and although they would send text messages and talk on the phone at times, it was not nearly enough to stay in touch like they were used to. Lindsay's smile was so bright when she saw Shaniqua and they hugged, and they examined one another. "Hey, you!" "What's up?" Miss Joanne smiled and admired the girl's bond, they really had something special, never any competition. They each wanted for the other what they wanted for themselves. Lindsay was dressed comfortably in a pair of levis polo short sleeve shirt with a pair of KDV by Nike. The girls rolled out to the mall after shopping and swiping Shaniqua's black card all crazy. They decided to grab something to eat at the food court. "So, please fill me in. Is New York what you expected?"

"Wow, true story it is huge and there's so much to get into. So many nationalities, diversity, and cultures. For example, every day of the week I can eat a different meal from another part of the world - sushi, Jamaican beef patties, pizza, gyros, girl. And it's true, the city never, ever, ever sleeps. People are always on the move. It's a lot easier for me now that I've gotten my studies out of the way, for the most part. Oh, and before I forget, I've been offered a position as an apprentice with a major law firm that covers every part of the law, from civil to criminal, with Johnson & Johnson's Law Firm."

'God, I'm so proud of you. So much has changed. You know how I've always believed in you, and truthfully, Shaniqua, you're capable of doing anything you put your mind to. Again, I love you, and I want you to keep going and pushing forward."

"Oh, you know I love you, Lindsay. You're like my hero. Don't make this a big deal, I'll start crying, and mess up my eyeliner," they both laughed. Shaniqua then slides a manila envelope to Lindsay. Lindsay looked at it and her eyebrows raised up.

"Open it silly," and she does. She was shocked to see fresh bills inside or crisp $100 bills. "Shaniqua, what's this for?" Lindsay asked surprised.

'Please take it, Lindsay. I know how hard you work and everything. Please, you never ask me for anything. Just always there, and you always have my back. Now please, take it it's a gift."

Lindsay saw a look in her best friend's eyes and gratefully accepted the money. The girls talked about other things and decided to go see a movie by Tyler Perry. After the movie, the ladies were tired and their feet hurt from walking through the department stores, so they decided to head to Shaniqua's house on the north side of Raleigh.

Both of Shaniqua's parents are home, and her father, Dr. Bradford, is cleaning and polishing his rifle in the den. Dr.

Bradford is an outdoors person. He loves to fish and hunt. He's just bought a new Chevy Silverado to haul his bass boat around. In the den, there's a pool table with a custom felt cover of the world map, as well as a full-size bar and mirror along the wall mirror covered in pictures of Dr. Bradford fishing for walleye, crappie, bass, trout, also pictures of him hunting for deer, moose, and bears. His last fishing expedition was in Costa Rica, where he went for billfish and a marlin. It was a challenge just to stay in the boat.

"Hello, Dr. Bradford. Oh, Lindsay, what a pleasant surprise. How are you? Still lovely, I see. How was school? I read about your track meet in the paper. You set a record!"

"All is well, thank you. School is good and thank you. I did run a lot better in my last race." Lindsay replied modestly.

"Always modest. I love that about you. Will you stay for dinner?"

"Yes, I will. Thank you very much."

Mrs. Bradford enters the conversation. She's the head of the household. Don't be fooled by her size. She's a tiny woman standing at 4'11, but she's strong-willed and spirited.

" Shaniqua, young lady, you will spend at least a full day with your father and I. You have been gone for a full year on your own. I'm proud of you, but you will not be a stranger in our home. We are family, so we need to catch up."

"Yes, Mother." Shaniqua answers smiling at her mother.

Shaniqua gives her mother a warm hug and then kisses her father on the cheek. She whispers to Lindsay out of earshot. "She wants to know if I'm having sex before marriage."

"What was that?" Mrs. Bradford asked, hearing her daughter try to whisper.

"Nothing, Mother." Shaniqua laughs and her and Lindsay lock pinkies together.

California

Diana barely makes her flight, and when she lands in Raleigh, her mother picks her up at the airport. She steps outside the airport and has her big shades on and sun hat to cover her eyes. She feels like crap and has a throbbing headache. Diana's wearing a zebra-print Roberto Cavalli maxi dress and sandals. Although she feels like she's been hit by a train, she still wants to look her best.

"Hi, Mom." Diana's mother helps her with the luggage. Her father couldn't be there; he's stationed overseas, directing U.S. troops in Fallujah.

"How does it feel to be home?"
"OK, I guess."

"Your father sends his love, and I made your favorite arroz con pollo. I'm happy to see you, baby, but I'm concerned about your grades."

"Mom, please, not right now, okay?" Diana replies sternly to her mother.

"All right, sweetheart." Diana's mother is easygoing and a bit of a pushover. Every week, faithfully, Diana's debit card receives a wire transfer of $500. It was $300 in high school, but of course, it increased when she began college at UCLA.

When Diana got downtown and saw all the traffic, she really let out a frustrated sigh. "What is all this hold-up?" Cars were bumper-to-bumper, and people were protesting, holding up signs that said, "Black Lives Matter." From the passenger side window, a little girl no more than seven years old was holding a sign almost as tall as her that read, "Am I going to be next?"

"The Attorney General Eric Holder is coming to Raleigh to speak about police brutality. A young Black male was shot several times last week; they say he was unarmed. It made national news. With the Attorney General being the first black US Attorney General, he can speak and add some comfort to the victim's family and calm the city's unrest.

"Dang, these people look angry. Mom, we should have taken another way home."

"I'm taking a fast route, Diana. Please be patient."

Diana ignored not only her mother but all the protesters as well. She grabbed her phone and began to text Lindsay and Shaniqua to let them know she was in Raleigh. Then, she scrolled through her phone, looking for someone who could get their hands on some good cocaine for her.

Mrs. Bradford prepared a full-course meal, and everyone was seated in the dining room. Dr. Bradford is proud of his daughter. Although Shaniqua was not following in her parent's footsteps and joining the medical field, she was pursuing a life-changing career in the legal field. As Dr. Bradford was aware, it is extremely difficult. Admission to most law schools is competitive and select schools may offer fewer than one out of four applicants a place in the incoming class. Normally, committee members, as well as administrators, make the admissions decision after reviewing the file of each applicant. The committee considers such factors as grades and performance by the applicant in college, the reputation of that college, and the applicant's score on the LSAT. Letters of recommendation and essays or personal statements by the applicant are also a plus. Again, very few law schools interview candidates for admission.

So together, the Bradfords are proud of Shaniqua's accomplishments thus far. Reaching her goals, the journey will be long, but she has done the hardest part by taking the first step. Instead of going out, a few family members and friends have been invited over to the Bradfords' lovely home for dinner and a quiet evening. Shaniqua had spoken with Diana and was asked to attend and expected to arrive before 7 PM. Shaniqua was looking elegant in a rayon mini skirt with side pockets, a belt by Mara Hoffman in matching peach Sleeveless blouse and metallic gladiator flats by Guess. Lindsay is dressed in something comfortable and elegant by Calvin Klein, and everyone is having a wonderful time. There are several children in the living room playing peacefully.

"So, Shaniqua, please tell me what type of law you're pursuing?" The question was asked by a cousin of Shaniqua who she hadn't seen in years.

"I'm interested in defense. I want to learn how to defend people who are in need and may be in an unjust situation. I want to make a difference."

"Wow, we need more people like you. What made you choose that field?"

Lindsay received a text message from Diana saying that she was on her way to the house. The reason Diana is running late is because, she just hooked up with a guy to score some drugs, and all he had was Molly. She has never done Molly but decided to give it a try to kick the withdrawal feeling . When Diana parks her mother's Prius in front of the circle, gravel driveway of Bradford's estate, she hears laughter and excitement from the home. Before going in, she opens the bag and takes another sniff, and then looks into the rearview mirror to make sure she doesn't have any white powder on her nose.

When Diana enters the house, she's extremely loud. "Hi everybody!" Her entrance does two things at once; it makes the women uncomfortable, and the men Google at her goodies. Diana is wearing white spandex and a shirt that stops at her belly button, showing her backside and every curve of her body. "What does she have on?" someone asks. Diana looks around and realizes she's dressed inappropriately for the occasion, with everyone else wearing sandals and shoes. She has on a pair of black and burnt orange Jordans Hoop TR 97's. Dr. Bradford can't help but look at Diana's shape and beautiful face. Miss Bradford is clearly upset, and if Diana wasn't her daughter's friend, who had slept over anrd eaten at their home many times, she would ask her to leave.

Shaniqua notices the tension and speaks greeting her friend while leading her into the kitchen. "Girl, what the hell are you wearing?"

"I didn't know. I thought it was just us."

" Us? I told you. And what are you High?" Shaniqua asked upset.

"Honestly, Shaniqua, you're my girl. You know I would never do anything to embarrass you."

"Diana, what's going on? Why are you dressed like you are about to go to a bike fest? And are you high? Look at your eyes, girl. Go to the bathroom and straighten yourself up," Lindsay takes control of the situation. When Diana comes back, she looks distressed. "My bad, I totally blew it," she says. "Come here, we love you girl. I told you, but it probably slipped your mind. Don't worry, it's no biggie," says both Lindsay and Shaniqua.

College and the party life were taking a toll on Diana. She had bags under her eyes like she wasn't getting much sleep, like a drug user. Lindsay thought to herself that she would try to talk to Diana one on one later. Now wasn't the time. The girls hugged, genuinely happy to see Diana after all. It had been an entire year, and they had a lot of catching up to do. Before leaving the kitchen, they locked their pinkies, as they always do, to show their bond, love, and affection for one another.

Chapter 5

The meal was great - macaroni and cheese, chicken, cornbread, fish, salad, oysters, cabbage, corn, rice, apple pie, and cheesecake. Lastly, after many discussions later, Shaniqua's love life is brought up. "So, Shaniqua, tell us about this man who is head over heels for you," says all the women simultaneously. Dr. Bradford is not smiling at all. "Come on, sweetheart, tell us, "He insists.

"There's really nothing to tell," Shaniqua claims while looking down at her plate. Lindsay is staring at Shaniqua so hard; she could burn a hole in her head. She thinks, We spent the whole day together, and she never once mentioned being involved.

"Okay, I'll tell it," Miss Bradford starts, looking at everyone. "So, I was at home from the hospital when I received a call from an obviously well-mannered, professional man who introduced himself and explained that he was calling to discuss an apprenticeship opportunity for Shaniqua at his law firm. He also asked for permission to meet with both DR Bradford and me to obtain our consent to take my lovely - and I emphasize lovely - daughter out to dinner.

At first, I was taken aback, as my daughter is 700 miles away from home and she's a grown woman. So, I asked him, 'Have you asked her?' He replied yes, and then he went on to explain that their meeting was strictly about the apprenticeship at his law firm, where Shaniqua would eventually share ownership, working side by side with himself and brothers.

As he talked, I started googling this man - and oh my god, he's perfect! No offense, babe," Mrs. Bradford says, rubbing her husband's shoulder. "I mean, he's older than Shaniqua by 15 years, but he graduated from Harvard Law with a Ph.D. in criminal law, served in the National Guard, played lacrosse for a sports team, has no criminal background or children, and is just an overall strong, positive, Black young man."

"Dr. Bradford interrupts, "Yes, I spoke to the man. He seems well-groomed, a handsome young man, but honey, it's not about us. It's Shaniqua's decision who she should date."

"Thank you, daddy. And we're not dating. He's God, I... mean..." Shaniqua can't even get it out of her mouth because Peter was everything.

"Where do I begin?" she says with a smile. And in a flash, she remembers the first time they met. Her professor introduced them, "Peter, this is Shaniqua Bradford. She is by far my most gifted student. Her zeal for law is impeccable I have to say, she would be perfect for your apprenticeship program."

"It is a pleasure to meet you," when he gently squeezes her hand, she melts, looking directly into his eyes. She noticed first his manicured hands, hazel eyes, wavy and groomed eyebrows, and pearly white teeth. His Armani suit and Salvatore Ferragamo shoes were on point. He stood 6 feet 2, muscular build, and when he spoke, he was so articulate with words. Later, he asked her for approval to consult with her parents about the program, which seemed weird, but she agreed. She ended up having lunch with Peter. Peter explained how at the firm, they were not just getting up and going to work every day but functioned like a family, of course, with him working alongside his older brothers. It was to him a real family business, with all employees and even clients. He wanted to have a close-knit relationship with them, so calling her parents was a way to also reach out to build a bond.

Now, Peter was impressed by Shaniqua's beauty. He saw her innocence and could smell the scent of a delicate flower waiting to bloom. Whenever he was near her: For a week straight, Peter sent yellow roses to Shaniqua's apartment. She agreed to go out with him one weekend, and it was amazing. First, she was picked up by a limousine and rolled in luxury, sipping champagne along the way to a five-star restaurant for lunch. They had gourmet cuisine dishes from Greece and

Egypt and red wine. After lunch, they were driven to the Ritz Carlton. Peter was the complete gentleman and allowed Shaniqua to relax and freshen up. She received a full body massage courtesy of the hotel staff, and the room service brought her a custom-fit Versace dress and shoes for the evening. The limo arrived, and they were escorted to the airport, where they then climbed aboard his private jet and arrived around an hour later, in Miami to enjoy the nightlife. Shaniqua was astonished by his lifestyle. They went to a few clubs and enjoyed live entertainment. Wherever Peter went, he was always the center of attraction with both men and women, and he was so natural with it. He never tried to be something he was not, and Shaniqua felt so comfortable with him. Never ever was he flirtatious or aggressive towards her sexually. Shaniqua was completely aroused by this man, and the climax of the evening was drinking a Grey Goose and cranberry cocktail aboard his 97-foot yacht, a beauty customized to suit his desires named Liberty. It was equipped with 316 L stainless steel hand railings. The Portuguese bridge had recessed stainless steel handrails and access to stowage staircase tread height and depth made for easy climbing. Custom wood craftsmanship aboard, even the helm wheel was book matched teak panels graced the interior. And again, Peter was mild and smooth, never violating her as they navigated from Miami to New York and docked in the Hudson River back in Manhattan.

"Tell us about him please, he sounds amazing," Diana inquired, bringing Shaniqua back to the present. "Oh, he's great, handsome, very intelligent," she replied modestly, not wanting to disappoint her father who was attentive with both his elbows on the table. "We're just friends, everyone, and yes, I've accepted the apprenticeship. It would be great for my career and allow me to get the experience I need."

"We're all proud of you, sweetheart," everyone agreed, and Shaniqua was glad when someone changed the topic. Diana was eyeing Shaniqua's cousin who came to visit and making sexual gestures toward him. He was handsome with a dark skin complexion, and she gave him the right eye contact to let him know that he had the green light. "Diana, can I talk to you?"

"Sure, Lindsay, what's up?"

"We need a heart to heart. How's school going?" After listening Lindsay could sense that Diana's interest for school was not as strong, nor her focus; it had changed, but she didn't want to seem judgmental or inconsiderate. "So, tell me about the bioengineering program."

Diana looked away, realizing she never mentioned changing her major to Lindsay and pursuing another career.

"I changed my major, I'm doing something else, but enough about me. How are you?"

Lindsay sensed the strain in Diana's eyes and knew it wasn't the time to push or argue, but she had in her mind that she would call and try to check on her friend more often. Lindsay told her about Fayetteville State and a few things about her new friend Natasha. "Don't worry, girl, can't no one take your place."

"She better not," Diana replied. Everyone was slowly leaving, fixing paper plates to take home, covered in aluminum foil, and Lindsay could see Shaniqua's cousin talking and looking like Tyrese in his prime, licking his lips, waiting around for Diana. Diana saw him and waved. He smiled, showing all his teeth, and Lindsay and Diana hugged, promising to keep in touch. "We'll be sophomores this year. Time is flying, right?"

"Yeah."

Six months later

Lindsay was on her way to her psychology class. It was close to 2 PM in the afternoon, and she was walking with a girl named Linda who knew Lindsay from class. "Lindsay, what are you doing this weekend?" Linda asked. "Just trying to catch up on classwork. What do you plan to do?" Lindsay replied. Linda explained that she and her sister were taking her sister's kids to the Asheboro Zoo, which had a forest exploration ropes course. The air hike course would allow visitors to complete a series of 23 obstacles with the help of a trained professional guide. "Please, Lindsay, it will be so much fun. All you do is study, and I see you don't do the club scene. This will be good for you, my treat. Please say yes," Linda said. "I'll think about it," Lindsay replied.

Lindsay had been studying hard, and her sophomore year was going exceptionally well, with a 4.0 GPA. This trip with Linda and her sister would, if nothing else, break the monotony of campus life. "Here's the brochure, check it out, tell me what you think," Linda said. "I will, I promise," Lindsay replied.

Lindsay was seated in her class, a prerequisite course taught by Professor Patrice Wainwright on optimizing perfecting brain fitness. "With up to 500 trillion synaptic connections, your brain is easily the most powerful machine in the world. Even more incredibly, this amazing machine is constantly changing through a process known as brain plasticity, and you can take advantage of this process to improve and enhance your brain's jaw-dropping powers at any age," Professor Wainwright said. Professor Wainwright spoke with such a low tone and tranquil voice that if you weren't interested in the subject matter, you would fall asleep in class. Lindsay enjoyed the class, so she was very buoyant, but her notetaking was interrupted by the vibration of her phone. It was an unknown number, so she was hesitant to answer the call. "Hello?" Lindsay answered. "Good afternoon, may I speak to Lindsay Jones?" the person on the other end asked. "Speaking," Lindsay replied. "I'm Dr. Clark at Saint Baptist Memorial Hospital in Raleigh," the person said. Before he could even finish, Lindsay thought about her mother, and she felt a feeling in her gut that something wasn't right. "Hello, are you there?" the person on the phone asked. "Yes, I'm sorry, I'm in class. Please hold on," Lindsay replied. She quickly grabbed her books and belongings and rushed out of the auditorium into the hallway, which was quiet. "OK, what's wrong? Please, Dr. Clark, tell me my mother's all right," Lindsay said. Dr. Clark took a deep breath. "Lindsay, believe me, I wish I could, but your mother Joanne is in ICU here at the hospital. We are trying to do all that we can to keep her condition from becoming worse." The tears began to fall from her eyes, and the world felt like it was spinning out of control. Dr. Clark could hear her sobbing. "Lindsay, when can you get here? I know you want to be by her side," Dr. Clark said.

"Yes, God, I'm on my way. It will take me several hours." Tragedy always seems to come at the worst time. Lindsay got off the phone with Dr. Clark and saw two missed calls from her mother's neighbor, Miss Mabel. After calling her grandmother and then Miss Mabel, she learned that her grandmother had been calling the house and got worried when there wasn't any answer. So, Miss Mabel went next door, knocked, and knocked, then tried the doorknob. The front door was open. She said she hated to invade her privacy, but out of concern, entered the house and found Joanne on the kitchen floor unresponsive. She at once called the police.

Lindsay planned to get back to Raleigh on the first flight out of Fayetteville airport. Lindsay took an Uber ride straight from the airport to the hospital. She had been crying for so long her eyes were puffy and saw the receptionist at the desk who was kind and helpful. Dr. Clark was currently with another patient but left a notice that Lindsay could have 45 minutes with her mother when she arrived. Lindsay could hear the machines and breathing apparatus that doctors had her mother hooked up to. Seeing her mother lying there on the bed with her eyes closed made her weak in the knees. The nurse assigned to watch Joanne and the other patients on the floor of the hospital was very cordial and sweet-tempered. "Sit sweetheart, hold her hand, talk to her. She will pull through; God will see her threw" she said.

Lindsay held her mother's hand and talked to her. She adjusted her pillow gently, and tears flowed and flowed. Lindsay fell asleep at her mother's bedside, and Dr. Clark authorized an extended visit for Lindsay. Dr. Clark woke Lindsay, and after she used the lavatory to wash her face and freshen up, they spoke in his office. "I know this is really hard for you, and your mother will pull through. If you recall, I spoke with several other doctors, and we've all been running tests and trying to wrap our minds around your mother's strange symptoms, the rare outburst of health deterioration, and the severe fatigue. Well, a close friend of mine who attended med school with me ran some blood work, and we've found your mother's condition. It's a rare disease known as lupus erythematosus or chronic autoimmune disease in which the person's immune system treats the body's own tissue as a foreign substance that produces antibodies to fight it." "How can she fight this? I mean, what can be done, Dr. Clark? Please tell me what we can do."

"OK, first let me explain the damage caused by the body's antibodies and how they may produce symptoms such as rashes on the face, headaches, fatigue, arthritic joint disease, heart damage, shortness of breath, and impaired kidney function. Now, Lindsay, the reason your mother has been up and down so to speak, where she seems to be fine and healthy and then in the worst shape, is because the disease follows a regular course of remissions and flare-ups and may often incapacitate. Over 1 million people (about the population of Delaware) in the United States suffer from lupus, and the disease strikes women nine times out of ten more than men."

"So now that we know the disease is there, is there a cure?" Lindsay asked with concern in her voice.

"Well, young lady, we have gotten past the most difficult phase in any treatment process. We've named the problem. Now, I'm going to ask that you be strong and patient because things will be rough ahead, and your mother is going to need your support. Here are some documents about lupus for your mother, as well as yourself. You will be provided with a treatment center in Chapel Hill with doctors who specialize in this area."

"Thank you so much, Dr. Clark. You have been such a help."

"My pleasure. This is what I'm here for. This is my calling, and I genuinely want to see your mother pull through and regain her strength. The lupus has been causing problems to her heart, giving her stroke-like symptoms, but her vital signs show that she's been responsive and just going to need a week to heal up. So, we plan to keep her for 5 to 7 more days, and you're welcome to visit as often as you like. And if you'll excuse me, I have another patient and family to tend to." Dr. Clark stands and gently grasps Lindsay's hand, showing her that he will do his best to make sure her mother receives the best possible care. Lindsay left the hospital feeling better, despite her mother's current condition. She thanked God that her mother was still here, and they were now one step closer to full recovery and conquering this disease.

The next several days were hectic for Lindsay. She traveled back and forth from home to the hospital, to visit her mother and in between, her grandmother's house, and school was out of the picture. She wanted to finish school, but the commute from Raleigh to Fayetteville every day without a car was impossible.

Her mother was up talking and responsive every day. She seemed to become stronger and stronger. Lindsay read as much as she could on the internet about her mother's rare disease. She learned that, as with most other autoimmune diseases, the exact cause or trigger for lupus is still unknown. Even though research has shown that the disease results when a specific set of susceptible genes are exposed to a combination of environmental factors, such as infectious agents, certain drugs, such as anticonvulsants, some penicillin and estrogen therapy, ultraviolet light, physical trauma, and emotional stress, it is still not known to medical professionals which of these factors set the illness in motion.

As days turned into weeks, Lindsay asked and paid Natasha to pack all her belongings and mail them to Raleigh. Since she wouldn't be returning, being a good friend, Natasha folded and boxed up Lindsay 's personal belongings, and made sure her things were taken care of, and mailed them.

Lindsay missed college tremendously, but she had to take care of her responsibilities. Although her mother was up and moving about, she was still out of work, and Lindsay had used most of the money that Shaniqua gave her several months back when they were at the mall. The money she was going to use to buy a used car, she was now using to pay rent, utilities, and medical bills that her mother was accumulating. After speaking with the specialists in Duke Medical and Chapel Hill, learning about the treatment they wanted to give her mother, a new drug with steroids and elements to help balance the disease, would cost several thousand dollars, even with insurance.

Lindsay and her mother Joanne spent a lot of time together, and they continued to grow their mother-daughter bond. One night, while looking over photos, Lindsay saw an old photo of her mother and a young man smiling together at a Raleigh city fair. Lindsay got angry because she knew she had gone through every single photo in the album and had never seen this picture. The Polaroid was stuck to the back of another photo. She wanted to know who this young man was.

"Mama, who is that man?" she asked, pointing to the picture.

Her mother replied, pointing to the picture, and putting her index finger as if to remove the man from the photo.

"Sweetheart, that's your father. This was the Raleigh State fair. He was 12 years old back then. That was a long, long time ago, but when I close my eyes, I swear it feels like yesterday," Lindsay was filled with shock. She took the photo gently and studied her father's features.

The next morning, Lindsay needed to tackle two important tasks. One, she needed a job, and two, to transfer her credits to a college closer to home. She was considering NC State.

Diana was extremely depressed. She kept calling Todd back-to-back with only the same results being sent to his voicemail. She would go to his home, but she couldn't remember exactly where he lived. Diana was in denial, but the truth was Todd was through with her. He was hot for her in the past, but now he had moved on to some different younger first-year students.

Diana was really disturbed also because of the monkey that she had on her back. She has no sure way of getting any cocaine now because Todd was her main source and supplier, and she hasn't been to class in a couple of days. This semester has been a drag. She thinks everyone is in her business, watching her, judging her. "You freaks don't know me," she thinks to herself. Diana is burning bridges. She has had two intense arguments with her mom about her weekly allowance, which as a result has caused her father to question where all this money is going. The last conversation caused Diana to tighten up on her behavior because not only did her father talk to her, but he flew unannounced to California to do it.

Chapter 6

Diana's professor, Professor Finkel, a short European older man with poke marks all over his face and who wore orthopedic shoes and talked with a squeaky voice, was wrapping up his lecture. "One of the most important of all human enterprises is undoubtedly philosophy. Throughout history, philosophy has served as a stage on which great minds have studied and tried to understand the roots of human knowledge and the purpose of human life."

Diana walked out of class only to bump dead into her father. "Hey, watch it.... Dad. God, Hola Padre. Como Estes?" Diana greeted her father, and although caught off guard, she was quick on her feet and at once took on the role of daddy's little girl. Even her voice changed. She hugged her father and looked over him. He was out of uniform but still had on his jump Boots shined to the point that one could see their reflection in his boots. He was dressed from head to toe in American Eagle apparel, and Diana looked around self-consciously because her father's embrace wasn't as warm as she expected it to be. By the look in his eyes, she knew that he hadn't come all the way to California for games.

Mark, Diana's father, was not only in the Air Force but was a decorated war veteran. He had two tours in Iraq, and was trained to conduct feats and goals that would decide the difference between life and death, not just for himself but for Thousands of other human beings. "Daddy, I didn't know you were coming," Diana said, trying her best to look normal when, in fact, she was incredibly nervous. Her father had never just popped up unannounced.

Mark looked over his daughter with a detailed eye, and after his assessment, he knew that for one, she smelled like cigarette smoke. If that wasn't enough, she was on drugs beyond the gateway drugs like marijuana. She was using hard drugs, and that answered a lot of his questions of why his daughter was failing and absent from class most of the time."

"Let's walk outside, Diana," Mark walked ahead of Diane and opened the door. The campus at UCLA was colorful and vibrant, with students heading to and from classes. Mark looked his daughter directly in the eyes and, with his arms folded across his chest, asked, "Diana, your mother and I are concerned about you and your behavior. Now, you know you can talk to me, so tell me, how is school going?"

"Fine, Dad. Mom must be upset with me, and you come out here to check up on me like I'm some little kid."

"Well, first of all, young lady, earth to Diana, I'm your father, remember, just in case you forgot. So, when you talk to me, speak to me with respect. You and I have never had any problems communicating. Also, I didn't come here from very far. I've been in San Diego for a couple of weeks now, and if you would have returned my calls, you would know that. And finally, your mother, who is and was my wife before we brought you into this world, we vowed to love one another till death do us part. So, your behavior is causing my wife headaches, and before I allow you to continue to manipulate and walk all over her, I came to inform you of some changes."

Diana was fully attentive now. "Dad, what's going on? Where is all this coming from?"

"Diana, cut it out, OK? I love you, but I'm your father first, and then your friend, but never will I be your fool. You're sliding down a razor blade into a pool of alcohol, and if you want to destroy your life, then you will do so on your own, not, with your mother's and my help."

"Destroy my life? I'm doing what I'm supposed to do. way out here, OK? My grades slipped a little. I'm just trying to make the transition."

"Transition? Diana Mi Hija, you've been at the school for almost two years, and I spoke with the dean. You're failing."

"What, are you spying on me?" Diana was livid and shot back.

"Spying on you? Are you serious? I bust my ass since you were born to give you the best of everything. I'm not going to sit back and watch you throw your life away partying and using drugs."

"This is my life. I'm an adult. You would know if you were around," Diana tried to throw in her last card about her father traveling and not being home often.

"You know what? That's not going to work either. And you're right, you are grown. That is why your mother, and I are going to start treating you as such."

"And what's that supposed to mean?" Diana said with her hands on her hips.

"For starters, I bought that car for you as a high school graduation present and even let you drive it here after getting it shipped from the other side of the United States. I thought you would appreciate that gesture, but instead, you try to deceive your mother and me by changing your major only when you knew you were failing."

"I don't have to listen to this. This is my life, and I can do what I want," Diana was heated and the truth flowing from her father's tongue cut threw her like a double-edged sword. "You will listen. I love you and care about you enough to know that you're an adult, and your mother and I will no longer contribute to demolishing your life. So as of today, you will no longer receive an allowance. Every week, you're an adult, and adults work, so I suggest you find a job."

Diana couldn't believe her ears. How could her father be so heartless he was really going to teach her a lesson. And still have pride and ego? Wasn't going to allow her to just accept her medicine, knowing that she was in over her head?

"And since you're a responsible adult, I've had your car towed and put into storage. When your grades are productive, your mother and I will return your vehicle. Until then, you work hard and prove that you mean what you say and say what you mean because truthfully, Diana, I'm disappointed in you."

Her father looked hurt, but he was also sure that this was the best decision.

"Are you done?" Diana asked, frustrated.

"Yes," her father replied.

Diana grabbed some books and, for the first time ever, turned her back on her father and walked away.

Several weeks later, Diana realized that even her mother was serious about her father's decisions. No matter how much she tried to convince her mother that Dad was overreacting, her mother wouldn't budge. The last phone conversation brought her mother to tears. Yet, she stood her ground and refused to send Diana money because truthfully, she was convinced that Diana was changing for the worse. Diana was cursing at her and calling her repulsive names. It was over. Her heart broke, not being able to cater to Diana's needs as she used to. Her husband's words played back in her mind. If you want Diana to crawl deeper into the hole, she's in then keep giving her the shovel, because that's what you're doing, that's what we're doing. Providing our daughter with the weapons and ammunition to kill herself. " She needs help, Mark."

"Yes, she does but sweetheart she has to admit that first it hurts sending her to rehab won't change anything unless she knows that she has a problem."

Diana had no choice but to change her lifestyle. No, the drugs didn't stop nor did the partying, but what changed was the number of men she dealt with and the turnover ratio. This morning, Diana and a new friend, Alexis, were out at Crunch Gym in LA. For the last half-hour, they had meditated, stretched, and hammocked. In the last 15 minutes for closure, there was a nap session. Diana wore a racer back top with leggings and a pair of Nike Lunar Eclipse in purple and hot pink. Alexis had on Nike low-rise tempo shorts that left nothing to the imagination. She had a beautiful backside like Serena Williams or Amber Rose. Alexis was 5'4" 138 pounds, with a mocha complexion, and green eyes, and was Cherokee and white. She was a socialite who had the best of everything. She was raised in Texas; the European side of her family was wealthy, threw old oil money. The other side of her family had generations of agricultural work and casinos in Arizona on the reservation. Alexis was eccentric about everything she did, and there was no shame in her game. She was only attracted to wealth and what your money could do for her.

"Diana, listen to every man, you need to be his eye candy. No man wants to really be with a woman that he can't go to sleep with and wake up to. So, that my dear, that is why we hit the gym, to keep everything we're supposed to be. Now, the number one rule to remember with being with me and my team is you get in the wallet or bank account first before you let him into your box period. I will school you some more, but let's get cleaned up and go shopping. Tonight, we will be surrounded by the upper echelon."

Diana had saved money over the years and still had a SafetyNet, but she couldn't in anyway keep up with Alexis in any way. Alexis drove a year-to-date cherry red Mustang with the eco-boost, which she didn't pay a dime for, courtesy of one of her many sponsors. Yes, a sponsor was anyone who contributed to Alexis's Come Up Foundation. Diana also noticed that Alexis only used a little cocaine here and there but stayed away from Molly and ecstasy, stronger drugs.

After several weeks of hanging together, Alexis persuaded Diana to take down the perfect catch. They have attended several parties and events over the weeks, and Diana has done something that she has never done before not having sex, with a man who is a potential suitor because technically, she and Alexis have explored the art of cunnilingus. There have been several nights and mornings where the two felines have been wrapped up in the bed sheets, their bodies melted together, rubbing, and tasting one another. The whole experience was a first for Diana. But for Alexis, she was just another conquest.

Alexis has opened Diana's eyes to a whole different world. Diana considered herself a diva, but with Alexis, she has learned to dress differently, talk differently, and slow down on drugs and alcohol consumption. "Drugs are not to be abused. We want to look our best and put all our competition to shame," Alexis states with emphasis. Diana is actually seeing results. At a particular gathering, she met an older and conservative man who, after hearing that she was attending UCLA and having trouble as far as transportation, agreed to lease her a year-to-date Lincoln Continental and make the monthly payments. So now, Diana is driving a year-to-date Lincoln Continental and following Alexis's rules. She has yet to sleep with Walter, her new sponsor, and he's like silly putty in her hands, always being a perfect gentleman in hopes of one day being able to lay with Diana. She just continues to dangle the carrot on a stick in his face.

Alexis, Diana and another young woman of the crew, Tiffany, who is 6'3, a Brickhouse with an athletic build and chocolate complexion. They were eating at an upscale Italian restaurant, Casa Apici. Tiffany was dressed in Dries Van Noten pants. The leopard print pants matched perfectly with the neutral pinstripe jacket and gold Manolo Blahnik from Khaite shoes. The restaurant could seat 60 people and had a Roman style theme to the place. They were going to try the citrus-curried mackerel with Taggiasca-olive-orange butter and spaghetti with Bottarga chili and lemon. "Ladies, next month, we must prepare for this major event."

Everyone was listening carefully because Alexis had a way with words. She would captivate and enchant you. "Where is the event, Alexis?" Tiffany asked. "New York City, where dreams are made. We are going to the NFL draft and after-party. Two things, we will be surrounded by new money and old money. Now, we must play the part, ladies, so we will have our hotels and all accessories in place. At the NFL draft, we will see who's going to sign the million-dollar contracts, and the after-party will determine who will spend the most for our attention." They were all smiles and sipped their wine while Alexis went into detail about the keys to taking down sports figures and, most importantly, digging into their bank accounts.

Several Months Later

Shaniqua was still living in New York, and things couldn't have been better. She was now wrapping up a 40-minute private class at a new pastime, Slash Workout, that Peter introduced her to several months ago, fencing on 225th W.

39th St. at the Manhattan Fencing Center. In just a few weeks, Shaniqua could see the results of her shape and cardio. She was really enjoying the whole sport because, for one, fencing was the furthest thing from her mind. She takes private lessons from an Olympic trainer. She has now learned many things, from how to wield a weapon, proper footwork, and parries to attack-deflecting maneuvers. She simply knows how to hold a weapon properly. While leaving the building, she was ecstatic to meet Peter for cocktails at The Rosemont, a jazz spot in the Bushwick section of Brooklyn. Peter and the bartender Greg were cool, and there's always a composed crowd. Loud music is a nearly nightly occurrence at the bar, with a rotating cast from Corey Wilcox and trumpeter Clynt Yerkes and singers and songwriters, always around. Also, there are regular film screenings. It's a diverse place that draws an embracing crowd. A kind of come one, come all mix of people, black, white, jazz lovers, festival girls dancing threw the bar with sunflowers in their hair. When Shaniqua reached the bar, she at once saw Peter standing there. He always stands out, handsomely dressed in jeans, blazer, loafers, and a polo shirt. Shaniqua seemed to glide to him and kisses his soft lips. "Hi," she said. "Hey, beautiful. How was class?" "I'm getting better," she said, glowing. "Greg, a bottle of champagne, please. Today is special." "Oh yeah, spill the beans, man. What's up?" At first, Shaniqua thought that Greg was pulling her leg, like he wasn't in on whatever Peter had going on. But after examining Greg's facial expressions and body language, she saw that Greg honestly had no clue. "I'll tell you all about it when you return with the house's best deal?"

"Deal," Greg agreed, shaking Peter's hand. Greg was laid-back and easy-going; he had always dreamed of owning his own bar, and with all honesty and hard work, he had achieved his goal. He had a signature drink that was extremely popular: a cucumber margarita. Lately, he had been experimenting with creating variations of the classic drinks from the 70s, such as the Harvey Wall banger and the Long Island Iced Tea, which were becoming popular.

While Greg was gone, Peter moved closer to Shaniqua. After months of being together, he had still not made love to her. Shaniqua was still drawn to him and captivated by him, like the first day they met, and she enjoyed his company. However, he would not cross the line, and at this point, she was beginning to question herself: **"Am I reading him wrong? Am I not good enough?"** But Peter always showed her that the only thing he wanted was what was best for them both, and he expressed that he wanted love and commitment based on something concrete, not just sex.

"Baby, you look so fine, so beautiful that it could entice the stars to fall out of the sky and land right at your pretty little feet. That's how fine you are," Peter said. He always seemed to know the right words. He just had a way of doing things perfectly yet allowed it to seem effortless.

Greg brought the champagne back and had a smile from ear to ear. He wiped his hands on his custom apron with the bar's name stitched into the fabric. "Well, don't keep me waiting."

"Yes, don't keep us waiting," Shaniqua added, with her heart-pounding and her hands beginning to sweat.

Peter said, "Shaniqua, sweetheart, you have been working exceptionally hard in your field, and your grades have been outstanding." Shaniqua couldn't look him in the eyes; she was still very shy around Peter. "Most law schools require three years of full-time study, some offer part-time programs holding classes in the evenings, which you have been taking while also working at our office. Almost all schools require the same basic courses in the first year, which cover contracts, criminal law, property, civil procedures, lawsuits, Torts, and constitutional law-- all the meat and potatoes. So, along with classroom work, most law schools offer clinical programs that permit students to represent individuals with, let's say, relatively simple legal problems under the supervision of a faculty member. So...."

eter reached to grab his briefcase, which was resting on the floor out of their sight beside his barstool, and he opened it, pulling out a folder. "Congratulations, Miss Bradford. Here, within this folder, is your first criminal case." Greg smiled and clapped his hands. Shaniqua was speechless.

"Wow, whoa, God, Peter," Peter touched her hand to reassure her. "Listen, I have all the details inside and as your Lawyer Shaniqua I will assist with the faculty membership, so you have me."

"But I've seen your schedule," Shaniqua said.

"Don't worry about that." "Let me open the champagne," Greg went to open the bottle.

"Whoa, whoa, wait, that's not it. Attention, everyone!" Peter spoke loudly, something completely unlike him. He even got the attention of the band and customers who frequented the place. "I would like everyone to witness the first day of the rest of my life." With that, Peter got on one knee and proposed to Shaniqua, asking her to be his wife. He pulled out a velvet-covered box, which uncovered a 5.5-carat emerald-cut diamond. Shaniqua was in tears as she said yes, and the bar erupted in applause.

Six months later, in Raleigh, North Carolina, Lindsay had officially been out of school for two semesters. She had to work full-time to support herself and her mother. Things were extremely difficult due to the lack of transportation and the frequent medical trips to the doctors. Her mom had to meet with doctors, and pay the medication bills with no insurance, but Lindsay never once gave up on her mother. That was not an option, even if it meant sacrificing track and college. She had found a job at Walmart but was notified two days ago that Walmart was cutting 7,000 back-office stores and jobs over the next few months, centralizing its invoice and accounting departments, and other things that Lindsay didn't have time for. All she knew was that she needed to get her driver's license and find another job. So today, she was back at the unemployment office, waiting for her number to be called so she could be seen by someone. The middle-aged white woman seemed very approachable as Lindsay sat in a booth across from her.

"Hello," the woman said.

"Hello," Lindsay replied.

"My name is Miss Martin, and I'll be trying to help you with things like receiving your unemployment benefits, as well as giving you advice and suggestions for future employment. Is that okay?"

"Yes," Lindsay answered several questions, filled out paperwork, and answered more questions until after 20 to 25 minutes passed. The woman suggested that Lindsay apply to become a correctional officer at Central Prison in downtown Raleigh, North Carolina.

"A correctional officer?" Lindsay replied in awe. "It's not that bad. I know several people who were leery at first, you know, with all the stories. But trust me, you have benefits and Time off with paid leave, and the prison is within commuting distance from your home, only a few miles away."

The first thing Lindsay thought about was how her mother would say that prison was for bad people. But she kept an open mind and took down all the information to follow up. She began to really consider working at the prison because it was an easy commute to work, the job availability was immediate, and she could still take a few courses online while working to continue her education.

Chapter 7

After reading about prisons on the internet and watching videos and footage about correctional work, Lindsay was actually and naturally nervous. She thought about the possibility of being locked in prison around violent criminals. Then she thought about the reality of life - where at least in prison you were around or interacting with those who have been caught or convicted of violent crimes. What about those individuals on the street who continue to commit crimes and haven't been caught yet?

So, after going over the thought of working in a prison for maybe a week or two, she decided to go on the interview. She was hired at once and began the process of having a physical and going through training. She was taught about the rules and regulations of the prison system, the chain of command, and so forth. Lindsay also was walked through the prison in regular street attire, along with another group of individuals who planned to start working as correctional officers. They were shown the facility from within the actual structure while the inmates were doing their time.

Walking through the prison gave Lindsay an immediate impression of the reality of prison. The inmates were strolling around, going to and from the chow hall (dining hall), and she saw that most of the men looked like they had never seen a woman before. There were also males in Lindsay's group, and they received rude stares or glares from the men incarcerated. The tension was definitely in the air. Lindsay saw that she could and would endure the challenge, not fully knowing why life had led her to working in a men's prison facility. Yet, she was determined to keep a positive mindset about the whole situation.

The man giving the tour threw the prison was thorough, and professional. He answered questions and offered advice when it came to the actual time for Lindsay and the group to step into a cell and examine it from the perspective of an inmate. She couldn't imagine herself being locked up. The guide giving was a decorator veteran who had served in the Marines, so his concepts and ideology of the prison system were very conservative. He showed everyone in the group various places within the cell in which inmates could hide contraband or a weapon and other things could be hidden. He tried his best to equip his group mentally for what they could face in the future to become the best correctional officers they could be.

Lindsay returned home and ate dinner with her mother Joanne. Joanne was a lot better and still attending her medical appointments so the doctors could continue to check her progress. Lindsay spoke with her mother and helped explain to Joanne how everything was coming along with becoming a correctional officer. Lindsay realized that one always had the option to become a criminal justice major, which would then allow them to elevate within the system from a correctional officer to a counselor and even a parole or probation officer, depending on your training.

"So, baby, tell me, do you think it's for you?" Joanne asked.

"Well, mama, it's convenient, and the pay is OK, but right now it's a steppingstone," Lindsay replied.

"That's all right. God has a plan for you, baby, and sometimes we have to go into the worst places to find our greatest gifts or talents, so just walk by faith, baby, not by sight."

"Next week, I have to go to some more classes, and in one of them, they're going to mace me."

"Mace you? Lord, not my baby," Miss Joanne said, trying to get up out of her chair.

"No, mama, it's a controlled situation. Where a group of people, including me, will be exposed to mace and shown how to properly use it so that way if we ever need to use it on one of the prisoners, we will know how."

"Oh, I understand now, but still, you tell them people, 'Don't make me come up there.'"

They both smiled and continued to talk about life in general.

"I'm so proud of you, Lindsay, and I wish things could be different. You have so much to live for and the world at your fingertips."

"Don't cry, mama," Lindsay said while getting up and hugging her mother. "I don't want to hold you back or ruin your life, Lindsay."

"Come on, mama, you're not ruining my life. We are going to be all right. I love you, and it's not your fault you're sick, Mom. You have always been strong for me, so I'm going to be strong for you. Please let me help you."

"I love you so much, Lindsay."

"I love you too, mama. I'm here with you."

"Trust me, sweetheart, you won't be disappointed."

Several Months Later

Diana was on Facebook sending messages to her new friend, whom she had met during the NFL draft a while back. His name was Amar Jackson. He was from Kentucky, played running back in college, attended the University of Louisville, and was drafted first-round running back for the Atlanta Falcons franchise. Diana was impressed with his muscular figure and remembered vividly the speech that was given at the draft when he held up his jersey number. The reporters mentioned, "For someone not completely comfortable in the spotlight, he has come to embrace it all - the speeches, the trophies, and all the tweets from his current 250,000 followers."

Diana couldn't help but admire Amar's style as he wore a Armani smoke gray suit, blood red tie, matching red snakeskin belt, and red suede shoes by Todd Ismail. Her juices flowed as he spoke, and she knew she had to have him. "It's like I haven't played football in years. I've been away for only a few months, yet I can't wait to get back out there, put those pads on and grind. I'm also the youngest Heisman Trophy winner," he said, smiling.

Amar had received 52 of 61 first-place votes from the AP's panel of media voters, and he had seen 163 points overall, more than twice the quarterback David Brown and runner-up Turner Watson. Diane and Amar hit it off good and exchanged numbers, and at this moment, they were discussing about Diana taking a trip to Atlanta. "Why don't you come this weekend?" Amar suggested. "I want to Amar but...," Diana replied. "No buts, I'm going to make the reservations right now. We're going to have a whole week to ourselves."

Diana enjoyed how Amar could take control and be a leader. They had never had sex, only conversations over the computer about sexual plans for the weekend. Even though Diana was ready to pull out all the stops and give him all the attention he wanted, Alexis was telling her to just keep it cool and not give him the goodies. She suggested leading him on and giving him just the right conversation to have him open. But as she said, "Do not, I repeat, do not sleep with him until he breaks you off some of that NFL check."

The media had mentioned that Amar had signed an eight-year, $70 million contract and moved into a luxurious home in the Buckhead section of Georgia. The home was built by Thomas Meyer in a Spanish colonial style. Even with its lack of color, the complexity of the arches the choice of stone, and the handling of the natural light added to the effect of the old colonial style of architecture, especially the dome structure of the home. The centerpiece of the entry-level was a strong yet gentle curved plaster stairwell that made the home so remarkable. The decorator and decoration of the home were unbelievable; no expense was skipped over or not thought of. The home was decorated with all state-of-the-art smart equipment. "Diana, I want you to come here, and unwind everything is arranged," Amar said. "I'm coming tomorrow. I want to be there," Diana replied.

CENTRAL PRISON

Charles Altidore has been incarcerated for seven years now. Waking up to another day in prison is still as difficult, as it was the first day his life was taken and flipped upside down. "Count time, Count Time!" the correction officer yells, causing everyone to stop what they're doing and be in their assigned area to be counted.

The prison holds over 7,000 inmates and is located in downtown Raleigh, North Carolina, in the heart of the city. It was built in the mid to early 1900s and has five levels and five floors, blocks A to H, which consist of dorm cells, two-man cells, and even one-man cells. This was an old prison, so the laws in effect were ruthless.

Charles has seen his share of issues; The predators and lowlifes tried him early in his bid, but he stood tall and showed that he was no animal. Although caged, he was still a man and would fight for the truth and what he believed in, and most importantly, die for his manhood. From within his cell, the view was just the worst; just walls to stare at, one could look out to see steel tables, but he did have a window. The outside looked so much better; sometimes he would throw bread to the birds. At times, he would even see people, but it was not a good sight because they were protesting and lighting candles and lighters to try to voice their opinion about the execution about to occur. It was the worst knowing that at any time you would be executed by the state for a crime you committed or accused of committing.

Charles can think back to when he was a free man and remember that he never thought about these issues. They weren't of importance to him. Yeah, he knew the police patrolled and locked people up, but he was never exposed to the in-depth magnitude of the whole prison process. And now being in and a part of the system, he had a change of view and perspective.

The officers prohibited one from looking out the windows while protesters were outside trying to stop an execution. So, though he could see people, not officers, but human beings free outside his window, it was bittersweet because they weren't ever happy when they came into view of his window. Which turned the whole experience sour. Now no man's land is where the police sat down.

The Officers sat down at the desk, in the cell block it was the only time you'd see a police officer or correctional officer relaxing except during count time, which was three times a day - 7 AM, 3 PM, and 11 PM, the lockdown time of the whole facility. There were 8 showerheads in the shower, 4 showerheads on each side. and for each showerhead, there was no privacy. One way in and only one way out. There was a metal gate on the top of the cellblock. 2 TVs one shown news and one for sports, only the championships games shown in the gym. Inmates were grieving about the conditions, so although they showed movies twice a week, administration were becoming more lenient with the TV. When Charles first came to prison, In the beginning he was only allowed one phone call a year, and that was on Christmas. Yes, Christmas day, and he would hope and pray that his family was there when he called because he was only entitled to one attempt. And if he did get to the phone, the call was only for 10 minutes. Charles still couldn't figure out how the system could be so cruel by not allowing men in here to continue to at least keep, or attempt to keep, a bond with family.

"Charles, man, let's roll out, bro," said Saul, his study partner. They were studying law together and trying to find loopholes and inconsistencies in their cases so that they could continue to fight for their physical liberation. In prison, it's very important you must watch and know who you call your friends and who you hang around with, because birds of a feather flock together and bad company corrupts good character. Charles would deal with Rich for legal purposes, and they both worked in the kitchen, so they had gotten to know one another over the years. Saul aka Rich was laid-back, quiet, and mostly kept to himself.

Charles was born and raised in Raleigh, North Carolina, and Rich was from Richmond, Virginia. So, everyone called him Rich. "Man, I wish we had someone that could go on the computer and get some of these cases for us. Charles, I'm telling you, your case is so cut and dry, man." Charles could hear the enthusiasm in his voice, and it gave him hope, but they still were missing all their tools. With North Carolina having a policy of having the ACLU (American Civil Liberty Union) working on the cases of inmates, it was a slow process. Closed-custody facilities gave up the law libraries, and as a result, inmates had no inexpensive way to work on their cases and learn the law. They had to just send the information to the ACLU and hope that they hit the lottery because truthfully, the volume of cases completely exceeded the attorney ratio who could handle your case with complete devotion. Now, of course, there were times when the Innocent Project would help vindicate someone of a crime, someone who was even on death row, and get them released from prison, those who were falsely accused of a crime he/she didn't commit.

"Man, this is frustrating," said Charles.

"Be patient, Charles. Trust me, we'll find a way. We've got your appeal, and we always have the M.A.R (Motion of Appropriate Relief)."

"Yeah, you're right. I need to stay positive because getting angry is not going to change anything."

"True."

"Okay, guys, the library's closed. The library is now closed," the officer announced, and they all walked out of the library after being patted down.

" You headed to the gym?"

"Nah, Rich, I'm going to fall back today."

"All right, cool. Catch you later. Be safe." They both bumped fist and headed in the opposite direction. Charles could still remember the very first time he went to the gym, in Central Prison. Essentially, going to the gym was the death walk. You had to walk around the corner of the building, G block down a flight of stairs, and there were no cameras. The place was piss infested with needles, drugs were being used, and individuals were being raped. It was a journey into the belly of the beast. Still, you had to go into another building and go up two flights of steps. The stairs were also dark because even when maintenance put a light bulb up, someone intentionally would bust it out. Now, at the top of the stairs were two doors that opened inward into the gym. The right door had a picture painted on it of a pair of boxing gloves, and on the left, there was a picture of pink panties, and women's undergarments. So, no matter which door you chose, you had to fight someone your size. The only difference was when you chose the door on the left, the door with the women's panties painted on it, you were fighting for your manhood. You then went through the back of the gym, up another flight of steps to the boxing ring, a real Olympic-size boxing ring. The gym had state-of-the-art equipment; the best taxpayers' money could buy. Charles had almost not paid attention, gone through the door with the panties until Rich reached out to him and showed him the door. He still didn't understand but went into the door with the gloves, and the next thing he knew, a convict named Cool walked up to him and said, "Hey Youngblood, you fight 3rd after those two over there Get Ready." "What? Who's fighting?" Charles was confused and asked, which prompted Rich to jump in. "Oh, he straight? He'll be ready? You said 3rd, right?" "Yeah, third." Another convict named Soldier said to Rich and strolled off. "Yo, what was all that about?" Charles asked, his face a little too close to Rich's. "Listen, bro, it's just the way it is here. Everyone boxes at least one time. Those doors dictate your fate. Here it's the law of the land, man." "Fuck that. No one is going to make me box. I just came to play a little ball and get some stress off." Charles was kind of loud, drawing attention to their conversation. "Rich, being patient because he was older than Charles and he knew how prison life could destroy a man. here you are, already locked up and now you're surrounded by different animals' men who prey on your every weakness and exploit it until you literally have nothing left, Rich was not going to let that happen, So Rich pulled Charles to the side and put his hand up to calm him down. "Bro, listen. We're not in the world anymore, we're in another world. And in this world, there's no room for weakness. Now take my advice... Box now on your own or fight every day for the rest of your bid. Many people went through those doors with the panties thinking that it was a game, but the freaks were on them for the rest of the stay period."

It was not just the words; it was that look in rich's eyes and Charles even in his feelings and emotions of anger could see the concern. He looked around and saw (The wolves) along the walls the faces of men who worked out every day lifting massive amounts of weights, and at night, raping and sodomizing young men. They blamed their mentality on the system. You could hear the same battle cry, "Fuck these crackers. Shit, they gave me all this time." They were all just really frustrated excuses because to rape anyone was a mental problem or behavior of the aggressor. But in prison, some guys even went as far as to say they weren't gay, although they indulged in homosexual activity. To them, the only person gay was the man being penetrated or giving fellatio. "Listen, kid, the choice is yours." Charles made the right decision and ended up boxing a guy around his height and size. Although he went 5 rounds, each round 7 minutes, he lost, but he wasn't looked at as a chump and he didn't get knocked out. He earned a lot of respect from the lifers and convicts that day, 'see behind the wall, you have convicts and inmates living by a different set of laws and principles. Whereas an inmate would do whatever the police say to do, just to go home and call it a day, And Convicts stick to the code. Charles was now on his way to being recognized and accepted as a convict, a standup kind of guy. Charles worked out and headed back to the block. One thing was very important in a penitentiary: mind your business, and that's what Charles did. He didn't gamble, when he played ball, he watched his mouth because in the heat of the moment, people say things they turn around and regret, and he didn't sweat the television. He also was his own man; he wasn't in a gang; he just did his time and focused on getting his freedom back.

Alaska

"Peter, I'm impressed. You're truly an outdoorsman," Dr. Bradford commented. Peter and Dr. Bradford were now headed back to the hotel after a three-day fishing trip in Alaska.

"Thank you, Dr. Bradford. I must say, you really know how to bring the fish out of hiding," Peter commented, smiling.
"Peter, please call me Dennis. You are my daughter's fiancé. You're practically family," Dennis said warmly.

Together, they were wrapping up a trip to the Kustatan River in Alaska. The weather and landscape were breathtakingly beautiful. Their guide Jack Newton had flown them in on a float plane to all the great parts of the river to fish for hours for silver salmon. They had really enjoyed themselves and had a chance to get to know one another. They also appreciated eating the fish as well, and the guide would clean the fish for them. On several occasions, Dr. Bradford declined and offered to clean his own catch.

"Dr. Bradford, I mean Dennis, sorry. This trip has been emotional," said Peter.

"How so, Peter?" asked Dennis.

"I remember coming to Alaska fishing with my father. And now, enjoying these last three days with you has been great for me," Peter replied, looking at Dennis with sincerity.

"Well son, I've had a tremendous weekend, and I'm looking forward to us doing this again in the future. Now tell me, you mentioned hunting. I do some hunting myself. What type of weapons do you use?" asked Dennis.

"I use many weapons; crossbows, bows and arrows, rifles. A .30-06 is what I used to use, but recently, I started using a new model rifle, the Ruger Gunsight Scout. The bolt action is .223 and .308. It's funny that you ask because I have a story this particular gun actually saved my life!" Peter said.

"Do tell the story, Peter. What happened?" asked Dennis.

"My brother and I were hunting a few years back for elk in Alberta, Canada, near Simonetta River. I was the only one carrying a rifle because Michael didn't have a game license at the time. We were about a mile and a half from my truck when we noticed wolf tracks and fresh wolf paws in the snow. We continued walking and saw a spot threw the woods where crows were eating on a dead animal. So, I loaded my rifle slowly as we approached. I wasn't thinking that we might come upon a wolf eating a carcass. Then, I heard this low growling and low sound, but I couldn't tell what it was because there was a big spruce blocking my view. So, I had no idea what was making that sound, that's when Michael yelled, 'Grizzly, beside the tree!' the bear charged straight for him. With no time at all, I lifted my rifle and fired from the hip, hitting the bear's shoulder. As soon as I shot, the bear it stopped chasing Michael and started charging at me. I shot again from maybe 7 to 10 yards away. It just kept coming.

Still, it kept coming, it swung at me, spraying blood everywhere. I ducked out of the way, and when I shot for the third time, the bear was no more than 3 feet away and we were now face-to-face. My gun was empty, it swiped at me again, but I could tell from his groans and movements that his arm was hurt. That's when the bear opened his mouth to bite me, so I shoved the rifle barrel down his throat it chewed on the rifle a few times and it had stunned it I believe, stopped him for a couple of seconds. I was stunned for a moment, but I backed up, and that gave me enough time and chance to reload and fire the final shot. Finally, the bear went off and died in the forest. "I'm sure you were extremely terrified," said DR

Bradford. "Wow, how is your brother? I mean not physically, of course, but mentally?" "Michael is fine, but we both now look at bears in general differently," replied Peter."

"Dr. Bradford and Peter packed their luggage and headed back to the East Coast. Peter's transfer flight was to New York, and Dr. Bradford was headed back to Raleigh, North Carolina. They agreed that the trip was a total success and that they would do it again in the future."

New York

Shaniqua was still blown away by Peter's loft. Shaniqua and Peter had decided, now that they were engaged, to get married and planning to spend the rest of their lives together. They would now live together, they both discussed the living arrangements, and Peter suggested that they also not have sex until the marriage was official. Up until now, they had only enjoyed some innocent kisses, but nothing more. Shaniqua walked barefooted into the kitchen, which had a bronze decor. The cabinets were lacquered bronze, the table was custom-made of fluted smokey glass and bronze trim, bronze suspended glass ceiling, smokey satin Mirror, bronze hardware, the seating was polished bronze leather, custom bronze, light fixtures reflectors with precious textures filled the kitchen. The view from the loft was breathtaking. Overlooking Manhattan, she was expecting Peter to return from the hunting trip with her father later. Shaniqua reflected on how beautiful her life had become with the whole move to New York, going to law school, and finding Peter who was in love with her. They would lay in bed for hours, and even with her hormones raging and aching for him to take her to bed and ravish her body, Peter was the perfect gentleman. They could and would talk about everything, and she shared with him her fears and desires. She opened to Peter as she had never opened to anyone before. Peter was a great listener and gave sound advice. Plus, she never noticed a wondering eye when they were out and about. Peter was considerate of her feelings, and the icing on the cake was the way he interacted with her parents. Her father and mother thought and spoke highly of him as well. Peter was just a great man and wealthy. For her last birthday, Peter had surprised her with a Cartier watch of 18-karat white gold and Rubellite and Diamond stripes. She never knew what to expect with Peter, but she could always count on it being the best quality. She was making New York her home now, although she didn't have any friends, she could call her own. She had associates whom she would have lunch with now and then, but most of the time, she spent studying law. Peter would often comment on her burning the candle late at night, but Shaniqua truly wanted to be her best. She worked extremely hard and was hard on herself. Shaniqua sipped some chilled champagne and ran her bath. The bathroom was custom in the master bath, with a tub and heated towel rack. The painted mirror panels over the wall were beautiful after Shaniqua shaved her legs and listened to Drake's music. She dried herself off and rubbed her body with body lotion and sat on an all-white Mongolian lamb stool, relaxing and breathing in the aroma scented candles. Eventually, her body was relaxed, and she laid back nude onto the canopy bed.

Peter had immaculate taste; the curtains were by Robert Allen, linen lined with Colfax and Fowler linen. At least eight scones filled the bed. Shaniqua couldn't ask for more in her life; in New York, it was fulfilling her dreams.

Shaniqua often thought about both Diana and Lindsay. They didn't speak as much but still stayed in touch. Being in New York, life was much faster, and since things moved at a more rapid pace, there wasn't much time to socialize like she used to. She still planned to involve them both in her Valentine's Day wedding, which she had been planning with the wedding planner. Peter was so supportive about things.

Peter's mother, Miss Debra Johnson, as she insisted on being called, was very standoffish. What seemed cold towards Shaniqua? Shaniqua is trying hard not to dwell on it and make the marriage work. Peter is truly worth it; he doesn't hide anything from her. Peter has mentioned that out of all his siblings, he is not his mother's favorite. He wouldn't elaborate or go into detail, but he would also go out of his way to make Shaniqua feel special.

Now, Shaniqua wants to involve Peter's mother, Debra, in the wedding arrangements, but she refuses to let her ruin their day. The few times Shaniqua was alone with Debra were awkward and uncomfortable because Debra was always distant, even though Shaniqua was always respectful and courteous to her elders. Shaniqua thought that Debra was just being overprotective of her son, but she couldn't shake off the feeling that something wasn't right. Shaniqua was self-conscious about it. Thinking to herself Did I do something wrong? Am I dressed inappropriately?

Despite her doubts, Shaniqua could always count on Peter to make her feel comfortable and encourage her to know that their love was strong enough to stand the test of time. They often went out together, dressed casually, and enjoyed each other's company.

Atlanta

Amar was casually dressed he and Diana went out to eat Downtown Atlanta. The city was full of energy and potential the weather was nice and vibrant, Diana enjoyed being with Amar in fact since her first visit to Atlanta they were inseparable, Diana had been living with Amar for 5 1/2 months, and in her eyes, he was her knight in shining armor.

Even with his training and football games, they still found time to be with one another. Sometimes Amar would get upset very easily, but Diana knew it was just the stress of being a professional athlete who wanted to be the best at what he did. Amar wore a cotton and nylon jacket by Tommy Hilfiger, wool cardigan, navy-blue Nautica T-shirt underneath, cotton blend trousers by Mac Jeans, and Wolverine 1000 suede boots.

All attention was on Amar. He was the starting running back for the Atlanta Falcons, and a few people walked up to him, asking for autographs and to be seen with him to take a picture. Amar supplied Fans with a few, but then to Diana's surprise he became rude, saying, "Please keep it moving, I'm with my girl." He squeezed Diana's hand and headed towards the restaurant with a quicker step.

"I'm thinking about something the coach told me," Amar said. "Expectations here are what they are." Coach Bob Towns had told him in a meeting alone in his office, making things absolutely clear that Amar must perform as a rookie and earn his keep. Practices were crucial, and the level of contact in the NFL was on another level. In college, you had a level of expertise, and then you stepped onto a field in the NFL where everyone is a professional, even down to the kickers, and it's a reality check. Plus, on top of all that, every family member wanted a piece of his $70 million contract. He was the meal ticket often receiving a visit from relatives he didn't even know he had, and some people always had to be around. It seemed like people always had there hands out. Amar tried to do the right thing. He moved his parents into a new home, even put both his sister and brother in homes with no mortgage payments and bought them all new vehicles. His accountant assured Amar that he would monitor and manage his money. Amar wasn't business-savvy, his duty was on the football field. Although the Falcons were 3 and 8 this year so far, he had rushed for over 1000 yards and had 7 touchdowns.

Chapter 8

"Amar, what's wrong?" Diana asked, sensing a change in his mood. Diana was learning him well. Amar's moods would swing, he would be up and happy and then down and out. It was weird at first, but Diana and Amar had been living with each other for a while and she could read him well. "Just anxious to play this next game," Amar said.

Amar and his team had a bye, and he flew out to be with Diana. He kept Diana pampered – manicures, pedicures, salons, and massage parlors - there wasn't anything mediocre when he came to Diana, she was his trophy. Amar had only been with two girls in his life sexually - one was his junior high school friend, and that was only kissing and rubbing, when her parents went out one weekend, he lost his virginity. But he and the girl had lost touch with one another when her parents moved overseas, and that was the end of that relationship.

Amar rubbed Diana's hand, and it felt so soft and warm. He looked into her eyes and smiled, showing all his pretty white teeth. "I love you, Diana," he said. She put her head down. Diana didn't know how to respond. Diana was experienced with men and knew Amar had potential, but he was young and inexperienced. She often wondered what would happen when he began to have lustful thoughts or a wandering eye, and she no longer made him happy. She tried not to dwell on it, but it was impossible. He was a superstar, and women threw themselves at him, but Diana had pulled all the tricks out the bag to keep Amar comfortable and solid as a rock. The sex was amazing. He was a professional athlete and didn't smoke and only drank occasionally, so his stamina was like a beast.

"Amar, do you think it was a good idea that I dropped out of school? I mean..." Diana trailed off.

"Diana, you're my woman now, and no woman of mine, must work or go to school. All I want you to do is stay home and take care of the house."

"So, you just want me in the kitchen pregnant and barefoot?" Diana stated. Amar smiled. "You said it". I'm not used to this, you know, just being cooped up in the house while you're away."

"Diana, stop it, OK? I don't want to argue. I'm going to provide for you. you understand?"

"Amar's tone changed and he had that evil look in his eyes again. He got like that from time to time, but she took it as stress from football and being on the road. She knew Amar really loved her. They ate their food and went to the strip club Magic City in her year-to-date 4.6 Range Rover. Diana didn't have a problem going to the club with Amar because it kind of spiced up their sex life. As soon as they entered the club, they were treated like royalty, with sparkling bottles and strippers accompanying them in VIP. This had been a pastime for them for over the months. They would get a few private lap dances, have a few drinks, and head back home to have wild sex.

Diana was cool with that, but tonight was different. Amar had not even asked Diana; he just brought one of the strippers home with them. In the car, Diana was furious, because it was one thing to have a little fun, but Amar was being disrespectful with his actions, kissing and feeling on the stripper. The girl was white, thick, and built like a brick house, looking similar to Amber Rose and gorgeous, shoot she had to be working at the predominantly black strip club. But Amar had crossed the line by bringing her home to their castle. Diana sat in the backseat, completely upset. He even had the nerve to play with her vagina in the front seat. What was she even doing sitting in the front seat? Diana thought to herself.

If Amar knew that Diana was upset, Amar didn't pay her any mind. They pulled into the driveway, and before the truck was fully parked, Diana was out of the truck. She stomped to the front door and fumbled with her key. Once inside, she slammed the door. Amar brought the stripper into the house, and she immediately sensed the tension.

"Is everything all right?" she asked.

"Of course, baby. You're with the best," he said in a sexy manner. Pulling her close and hugging her. Amar dug into his pockets and pulled out a roll of Benjamin's peeling several off, "How much you need?"

The girl smiled like she was on camera and laid on the charm. "Oh, Amar I always wanted to see what was under that uniform". He led her to his guest bedroom, which was decorated and equipped with a flatscreen hundred-20-inch television and a Jacuzzi.

"Sexy, take a bath, get comfortable. I'll be back," he said. There was no question whether she was staying. She just knew she hit the jackpot. "OK, I'll be waiting."

Amar left her in the room, and his whole demeanor changed. He walked up the stairs to the second floor of his house, to the master bedroom. Diana was in front of the vanity mirror, removing her eyeshadow and makeup. Amar was visible to her through the mirror. Without words, he walked over to her and smacked her backhanded over her stool. She hit the carpet hard, and he rained his fists down on her. She yelled but couldn't get through to him.

"Amar Stop... OH stop. Oh God, stop! It hurts!" she cried.
"Bitch whose doors you slamming? you're my woman, and you're going to respect me," Amar said. Diana was in so much pain. Finally, the blows stopped, and Diana crawled into a fetal position, crying her eyes out. Amar did not seem to have any sympathy. He just went back down to the guest bedroom

and had sex with the stripper for several hours. After calling an Uber for the stripper, he went upstairs and got in bed next to Diana. When he touched her, she jumped. She was so startled and confused. Amar talked to her as if everything were all right. "Baby, I'm sorry. I got a little upset. I love you. I just want to make you happy," Amar said to Diana. She was scared and confused, never having experienced this kind of behavior from anyone before. She wondered if she had done something to provoke him. Despite everything he had done for her, she didn't know what to do. Diana knew he loved her and had done so much for her. Her face was swollen and bruised, and her body ached but Amar climbed on top of her and before she knew it, he had emptied his seed into her.

Central Prison

Lindsay was a little nervous with this being her official first day working at the prison. She was self-conscious about her uniform; her pants were kind of tight which hugged all her curves that she had inherited from her mother and grandmother. Once she arrived at work, she used the restroom and popped a piece of gum into her mouth to calm down. She saw a familiar face, one of the officers she had trained with, Mr. Cooper. He was cool, tall, muscular, and young. Lindsay noticed his eyes roamed over her body, but he kept things cordial and professional.

"Hey, Lindsay. Are you nervous?" he asked.

"A little," she replied honestly.

"Don't be. No need to worry. Everything is going to be fine," he said reassuringly. His size alone made Lindsay feel more comfortable.

They would be working the same rotation, and during the intake routine ritual, the captain or lieutenant would explain to the following shift what they had to do, as well as what had occurred the previous day and the department's goals and objectives. The Department of Public Safety (DPS) was big on officer safety, and it was imperative to take every precaution to protect the officers as well as the inmates. But truth be told the officers were outnumbered and in constant danger behind the walls of Central Prison, there was a history of violence there were laws and rules that one could not find or read about in the policy and procedure manual. They were written in the minds and hearts of the officers, who protected each other and stuck together no matter what, right or wrong.

This particular captain had been in the system for over 20 years and had seen it all. Nothing surprised him, he had seen riots, medical issues, murder, insubordination by officers, and corruption. You name it and he knew it existed. He was a decent man, a family-oriented person, and even convicts and inmates had respect for him because, if nothing else, he was fair.

"How's everybody feeling this morning? Hope everyone is rested. We plan to have a regular routine shift today. Nothing special going on. Let's watch each other's backs and have a safe shift," the captain announced.

Lindsay situated her walkie-talkie, security stick, mace, and gloves. The butterflies were still in her stomach as she was patted down and went through the metal detector. Now she was headed to her cell block (K-Dorm) as soon as she walked through the tunnel. All eyes were on her.

"Damn little mama god damn" One of the inmates commented "Oh yes Sexy Chocolate" It was cat calls from a few idiots, and she kept it moving into the cell block. The first thing she noticed was the smell; the block smelled like a gymnasium and a septic tank mixed. God, she thought to herself Lindsay got herself together to relieve the officer on duty. She put her belongings into the cabinet and adjusted herself, her first duty was to walk around the block and make sure everyone was, for one alive and then make sure rules were being followed. Lindsay began her lap around the block looking into every cell some men were sleep, others praying, she even looked into one cell and saw a man completely naked stroking himself Lindsay was shocked because she felt like she was invading his privacy, so she kept going like nothing happened everyone was accounted for, and no one was fighting. So, she was straight. Lindsay sat at the front desk and several men came and asked for paper or envelopes, or the newspaper and then a man wheeled up in his wheelchair when no one was around and began asking a lot of questions. Questions Lindsay did not care to answer. Lindsay wanted to be courteous because he was in a wheelchair, but his questions became vulgar and inappropriate, so she asked him to leave.

The men went to breakfast and before lunch she had a break 20 minutes to use the restroom etc. and was relieved by another officer the female, she was working with was just as happy as she could be her hair was done so were her nails and her pants was skintight her name was Miss Watkins "Hey girl how was it so far for you? You, OK?" "Yeah, I'm cool" Lindsay replied. "YO BE ON POINT WATKINS ON DECK" One of the younger inmates yelled throughout the cell block. One of the Inmates went into the shower. "These Niggas are fine aren't they girl?" "What?" Lindsay answered. Lindsay was green and didn't realize Watkins was the type of officer who floated around the prison sizing inmates up and was even in relationships with a few different inmates in different units "Oh girl please don't try to tell me you ain't seen nothing you wouldn't let hit that.?" "Oh no I'm good" Lindsay said offended. "I feel you; I get it." Ms. Watkins knew it was her first day and she was not trying to make an enemy.

Ms. Watkins switched out with Lindsay and an hour later while Lindsay was in the control booth operating the doors and watching the cameras, she saw Ms. Watkins walk into an inmate's cell now at first, she wasn't paying any attention she just assumed that Ms. Watkins saw something in the inmate's cell. That he should not have but then she saw an inmate about 6-foot 4 muscular man with his shirt off come out the shower with his pants legs rolled up, he had all these tattoos and walk like he was the owner of the place. His swagger was different. He entered the same cell that MS Watkins was in. And she did not come out for 25 minutes and when she did, she was fixing her clothes. Lindsay stayed in the control booth for several hours until she got a break and returned to the floor, to relieve Ms. Watkins she seemed worn out and tired "Girl I need my break!! Damn I'm tired" she said walking away. Lindsay sensed an undertone to her statement, but she really did not want to read into it too much Lindsay made her round, sat at the desk, and watched the block. Lindsay noticed that a lot of men were coming in from the yard or gym and rushing to the showers.

Showers were on the east side of the block with six showerheads on Each side one way in and one way out. Some inmates went 2 at a time and looked to be guarding the shower looking out for each other holding it down for one another. One man would stand outside the shower keeping anyone from entering while the other man showered. Lindsay looked and saw one man in a shower with another man they were ignoring one another but in another shower the curtain was pulled back, and a young guy was in the shower looking directly at Lindsay. Why? she said to herself. While Lindsay sat at the desk, and he began to masturbate She immediately turned her head. Now she had been warned about this and was told by her supervisor to write anyone up that she saw doing this, but she was really confused thinking should I even be looking in the shower while these men are in the shower. Lindsay looked again and now his muscular figure was in Full view and she shifted in her chair, uncomfortable she witnessed him stroking his erect penis comfortably and he kept going until he climaxed, Lindsay turned away.

Telephone Conversation

"Oh my God Lindsay I'm thinking jimmy Choo Heels classic black Tuxedos filet mignon and lobster you know how I love seafood" Shaniqua was describing her dream wedding which was only a few weeks away Lindsay and Shaniqua were talking over the computer Lindsay would of course be the maid of honor along with Diana but Shaniqua had asked Lindsay first not out of favoritism but truthfully Shaniqua and Lindsay had a very tight bond "I'm so happy for you Shaniqua a Valentine's Day wedding you go girl have you spoken to Diana?" "Not yet do you know how hard it is to get up with that girl?" "I agree" Lindsay replied because ever since Diana started living with Amar Jackson in Atlanta it was like she disappeared, but she seemed so happy the times they did speak on the phone. Amar this....and Amar that... "God is good they seem perfect together and shoot it doesn't hurt that he's worth $70 million" Shaniqua said "You're right at least she's happy but you know how I feel about education Shaniqua she should've never dropped out of school. Not to throw shade but what happens if things don't work out for them then what? Diana won't have anything to fall back on. they've been together for about a year, and they aren't even married I don't like Diana shacking up like that" "I agree but Diane is grown and has to make her own choices!" "you're right how's miss Joanne doing?" "She's doing better they have started giving her steroid shots now so she's able to go out more we actually went to the grocery store and went shopping together the other day it felt good to see my mother walking around on her own" "Oh Good thank God Lindsay I'm so proud of you Lindsay I admire your strength girl how's the job going? because you know I worry about you being in that prison with those men" "It's all right I'm trying to get moved to another unit with another crew" Lindsay says sounding upset "Why what's up?" Shaniqua asked listening carefully. "So, you know

I've been working almost 5 months and I'm into my routine good minus all the extra stuff coming my way I'm all right, but I work with this heifer who is trying to play on my intelligence" "Who? Oh what's going on?" Shaniqua wanted to know." Her name is Watkins, and she is loose; she's having sex with this guy and bringing him drugs and it's gotten so out of hand that some guys were fighting the other day and one of the men was stabbed in the back really bad" "What so quit, I don't want you around that. You and Miss Joanne can come stay with me, we will work things out" Lindsay could hear the concern her friends voice "No we can't Shaniqua but thank you , and I can't quit" "But you must tell on her to get her fired" "I can't do that she has kids and even though I know what she is doing is wrong two wrongs don't make it right Shaniqua., I'm in the process of getting transferred to another unit in another part of the prison." "What if someone gets stabbed again?... Are the men being stabbed in that part? God, I don't want you around that." Shaniqua was crying over the phone now "Don't cry" "I can't help it Lindsay why do you have it so hard?" Shaniqua sobbed "My grandmother says she prayed for me and ask God why I always go threw troubled waters? and God told her because my enemies can't swim. So don't cry things will be all right and enough about me I'm coming to New York to see my sister get married to the love of her life now stop that crying before I come through this computer and tickle you to death"

Lindsay said they both laughed. And Shaniqua brightened up. Shaniqua was thinking about her husband to be Peter and how he told her over and over "Baby this will be a day to remember, here's a blank check do with it as you please. Our union is priceless so there is nothing I wouldn't do or give to make you happy." Shaniqua was thinking to lease the ballroom of the Ritz Carlton which featured a private foyer for cocktails before dinner and is located in the heart of the city which combined elegance and style or the Ballantyne Hotel and lounge it had gardens, fountains, and a iconic grand staircase that was picture perfect for the photographs "God there's so much to choose from I'm sending 300 invitations that includes Peters family and friends as well as us. The wedding planner has really been giving me hell, but I just want everything to be perfect. OH, Lindsay am I being selfish?" Shaniqua asked "No This will be a day for you to remember the rest of your life take all the time and planning you want and if it's anything I can do to help please let me know" Lindsay assured her.

Shaniqua thought about the guest having a panoramic view of everything across the New York city skyline being so many stories up. The multi layered cake, snacks, and refreshments for the guest. A horse and carriage to bring both Peter and her to the event she wanted everything in all white, her wedding would be pure the indoor venue would have everything to make things classic yet fun and unique popcorn and dessert bars as well as hors d'oeuvres "Have you chose a wedding dress yet?" Lindsay asks, "No, well, I have one in particular that stands out. Its the 1950s-inspired Tulle- tea-length ballgown. It's amazing, Lindsay. Trust me, you'll love it" Lindsay could obviously hear the excitement in Shaniqua 's voice. "It sounds like the one you should get it." " I hope so , you think? wait I'm going to send you a picture Lindsay I want you to come a week before my wedding and stay with me so we can go out and enjoy ourselves" "I already put in the vacation time with my job for time off I'm just getting things situated for someone to watch my mother while I'm away" "Lindsay don't worry about anything I'm going to pay for all your arrangements OK and Peter has a brother his name is Michael that I want you to meet" " Listen   hold .. Up matchmaker it's your wedding girl understand? Now do not go trying to push me down the aisle next.". They laughed and discussed old times and tried to get caught up and before they knew it several hours have passed and just like when they were young, they were exhausted and fell asleep right after they ended the call.

Trip To Charlotte NC

Diana was applying a few more spritz of modern mousse perfume by Estee Lauder she was flying to Charlotte

North Carolina to meet with Alexis, they haven't seen each other in months and Alexis was feeling some type away because for one Diana was no longer in school matter fact she dropped out and was living with what Alexis called a sponsor. So, talking over the phone was out of the question Alexis needed to speak with Diana face-to-face because Diana 's membership to Alexis 's club was in question as well as their friendship. Alexis was zero tolerance when it came to following sorority rules loyalty was a must and trust was expected so the ladies agreed to spend a weekend in Charlotte which was convenient for Alexis she had to attend an event in Charlotte to support one of her sorority sisters as well as entertain some potential sponsors so luggage was packed for the weekend.

Alexis bought everything from Chanel, Louis Vuitton, Dolce and Gabbana and Versace for Safe measures. When Alexis stepped out, she was always on her (A) game. No exceptions to the rule. Hair and nails done, and Alexis had a glow from the tanning salon. Now Diane on the other hand was in Bankhead waiting on a guy she met one weekend while out at Walmart she was surprised she even took his number because if Amar found out there was no telling what he might do. Amar had become more abusive now, he would cuss her out call her names he even would flinch or act like he was going to hit her if she did something wrong, like leave a plate in the dishwasher or sink if his food wasn't ready on time the bed wasn't made tight enough.

Diana needed a break and although she had quit using drugs for several months because looking back everything was perfect between her and Amar, they were on top of the world he was so gentle, soft-spoken, and kind but ever since they started having sex and living together Diana 's life changed. Amar was a completely different person, so Diana decided to go to Charlotte to be with Alexis and clear her head. Amar was on the road playing football so she would try to have an enjoyable time now here she was in the heart of Bankhead Atlanta driving a $100,000 luxury vehicle waiting for a guy name Night looking to score some cocaine. Diana had two fresh $100 bills Night pulled up in a Cadillac on 32-inch rims and got into the truck Diana was driving. "Wats happen in Shortie?" Night spoke with a southern accent showing his mouth full of gold teeth. "I'm trying to get straight you got something?" "Yeah, I got you but first wats up with me and you?" Night asked squeezing Diana's thigh she flinched it had been uncontrollable Amar had Diana so on edge that she found herself jumping at any touch "You Kool and all Night but I'm on my period it's not a good time for me." Diana was quick on her feet and did not want to hurt Night's ego so she lied but Night had a look in his eyes that he did not care he would still have sex with her if he could." "So how much you got shortie?" Night dragged the word Shortie; with his southern drawl she gave him $200 he took it from her hands and pulled out two balloons which were mixed with both boy and girl cocaine and heroin. They made the exchange and Night squeezed Diana's thigh a little bit longer before getting into his vehicle and driving off. Diana did not waste any time she ripped into the balloon and stuck a straw into the pile of badge powder and sniffed until she could feel the poison draining down her throat and it numbed and took away all her pain.

Alexis arrived in Charlotte at the airport smelling like Coco mademoiselle pulling Louis Vuitton luggage there was a chauffeur and stretch limousine waiting for her, to take Alexis to the hotel. Alexis sipped champagne in the limousine and talked on her iPhone with one of her sisters from her sorority about the events for tonight. The party was a lingerie theme and an auction after the dinner banquet, there would be a lot of old money present since the organization started in September 1962 it held quite a few events including a fashion show, celebrity basketball game and events for the kids, yet the adults also wanted to have discrete alone time to play and that's where Alexis came in. Alexis provided the sexual entertainment these people were upper echelon supreme clientele. Consisting of Lawyers, Judges and Doctors and even an oncologist and they had their fetishes. And their anonymity was imperative. Alexis had a suite at the Ritz Carlton and all seven of the women including Diana met there the ladies were pampered and treated like luxury.

Alexis had brought her top seven horses which ranged in all shades from ivory white to Cocoa Brown and even deep rich sun kissed chocolate these women were in the business of making money and their desire was to please. Alexis was professional with her system and all transactions as for finances were pre-arranged and digitally transferred to different accounts.

The women were dressed conservative for the start of the evening one particular client was drinking Top Shelf Don Julio straight from Mexico and with his ice blue eyes and tailored made suit He seemed relaxed, so everyone could tell that he was extremely wealthy. His name was Dr. Grizel he was a plastic surgeon, a highly trained surgeon and was board certified by the American Board of plastic surgery using the latest surgical techniques and minimally invasive procedures. And was proud to serve as chairperson of the plastic surgery of Novant health now behind the scenes he had a thing for mixed or biracial women to tie up and spank, so he was used to getting what he wanted, and he normally did. Most people didn't have the heart to tell him no!

The guests enjoyed basil Thai lamb, Alexis ate the red curry Duck it was deep fried dipped in a spicy red curry sauce one of the older men was admiring the way Alexis was wearing a white Vince Camuto lace dress and brown Kamaye lace up sandals, especially with the fact that her areolas were showing clearly for everyone to see. Diana was also standing out amongst the others wearing a Dior Haute contour suit with a Cartier necklace the black suit with white stitch open to show her cleavage was amazing, there was live entertainment, and as the temperatures began to rise the ladies headed out to the rendezvous point to get the real party started. All the men seem to drive luxury foreign vehicles Mercedes, Porsches, Ferraris, you name it, and it was there.

The limousine transported the women and parked on the gravel driveway at 50 O'Toole Stone throw Court in a suburban area of Charlotte before them with the stars shining view of the full moon bright. Was a three-story brick home exquisite luxury living. Full brick custom built home, Wonderful floor plan, The home was equipped with home theater, Billiard room, built in elevator,2nd kitchen, marble counter tops 8 ½ bedrooms 2 full bathrooms and a garage parking for nine cars superior craftsmanship abound from the gourmet kitchen to the 1400 bottle wine cellar this magnificent home was worth over $25 million

Alexis and the other women were led into the home by security two big body guards both looking look like all they did was train and lift weights muscles on top of muscles. Dressed in tailored made suits, the women walked into the foyer. All the women were amazed all except Alexis she was a Madame used to the luxury of being around extravagance. Alexis had been cold towards Diana and short with her words, it was obvious that they needed to talk. with Alexis was business first always they could discuss their differences later, the ladies were led to the den and the fireplace in the middle of the room brought warmth and comfort the men were dressed in expensive robes solid colors it was champagne on ice and cocaine laid out for anyone's use. Alexis led the women to change clothes and when they returned all the women were dressed in lingerie by Victoria's Secret.

Three men led Diana down to the basement she hesitated at first because Diana had not been informed or paid for this service Alexis neglected to tell her what type of party or situation into which She was getting. Alexis saw the concern or was it fear or confusion in Diane's eyes? but ignored it and gave Diana a smile phony but a smile at the least. As the men took the elevator down to the basement Dr. Grizel was the main leader to escort Diana to the basement and he had special plans for her as well as the two men with him Dr. Grizel was a pain-freak he enjoyed giving or administrating pain. Diana was blind folded put in handcuffs and gagged with her hands overhead naked. With different hands groping her probing and pulling on her nipple clamps were applied and pulled repeatedly to her nipples. Oil was applied to her anus. when the whips and canes struck her backside, she came to tears. As for the other women it was sounds of love making and animal Sex everywhere one on one, two men with one woman. Alexis was entertaining a young man whose father owned the establishment and the young man was being taught the art of cunnilingus until Alexis had enough. Alexis was smiling to herself in a conspiratorial way with the thought of being paid to have her clitoris stimulated what a life.

Hours Later

Diana felt like she was in a train wreck her body ached she had been stretched with dildos and full of semen in all her cavities. she felt humiliated. Alexis lied to her and had told Diana that she and a few of the sisters were to have a nice evening and model lingerie for some old potential sponsors. Now here she was confused being used by three strangers. she wanted to take a quick shower and try to clean herself up and wash the filth away. And clean away the way she felt she cried in the bathroom. Alexis was not a friend how could she do this? Diana felt like she was worthless and the bruises on her body from the cane and different whips that were used all over her body looked like she was in a fight. Diana was so upset she would try to fight Alexis yet; Diana was no fighter, but she would give Alexis a piece of her mind once dressed and fully clothed because Diana could only wash up unable to shower, Dr. Grizel saw the look of anger in Diana's eyes and his smile vanished his face turned red. DR Grizel asked, "What seems to be the problem?" He was confused himself; he enjoyed his fetishes but not with unwilling participants he asked again in a firmer tone as Diana stepped into the elevator. Tears running down her face. "What, where are you going? I paid for the whole weekend?" He stated and Diana smacked him as hard as she could before she pressed the up button on the elevator. He was shocked as the doors closed in his face.

Diana burst into tears, hearing the revealing truth that DR Grizel had paid for what those men did to her. It all seemed to give her a new pain Diana found Alexis and screamed at her "How could you? How could you do this to me?" Alexis couldn't look Diane in the eyes and stated Coldly "If you were leaving then your services are no longer needed and someone will retrieve your luggage from my hotel, I don't want you returning to the room I don't trust you" "You don't trust me? Me you bitch!! I can't believe you did this to me I thought we were friends" "You broke our friendship when you disobeyed the rules" Alexis answered sharply. "Rules? What Rules?" "Diana was Livid. "I told you not to sleep with them That included Amar Jackson "Alexis emphasized with her hands. "You were told not to do so and what did you do? You dropped out of school and even had the audacity to live with him. Now you are dismissed I don't even want to see your face again." Alexis looked at her with disgust "You know what? fine I'm not your child Alexis and what you did was hateful and wrong." Diana wept and she walked out with her belongings the driver took her in another vehicle to the hotel she waited in the vehicle and then her things were brought to her. Diana was taking to the airport. Diana had a layover because the flight out of North Carolina was in three hours, so she went to the bathroom after booking the flight and used the rest of a supply of cocaine which was mixed with heroin.

Atlanta

Once back in Atlanta, she thought she would unwind and have the house to herself, but wow was she wrong. When she stepped into the home her heart dropped there was Amar sitting on the couch in the dark obviously Hot and upset about something. "Amar I wasn't expecting you what are you doing here?" "What... what am I doing here? I live here remember" Amar said sarcastically "Now tell me where you have been?" Diana was stuttering in panic because she hadn't been able to come up.

Chapter 9

With a lie or someone to vouch for her absence plus she smelled of sex because she had not taken a shower since the session or ordeal rather with those three strangers "I... I was" Amar cut her off. "Don't lie to me Diana" Amar grabs her arm and squeezes hard enough to bruise her "I was out Amar that's all I needed to clear my head" "Clear your head for what? here I am busting my ass day in and day out to support you. My team has a buy, I fly in to surprise you spend the weekend with you, and I come home to an empty house" Amor was irate now swinging his arms around Diana hated it when he got like this. Then he was in her face spitting and screaming and he grabbed her by the neck "Now where were you?" "I was out Amar" Diana answered scared he smacked her across the face she fell to the floor crying "How? Did I give you permission to go out?" Before she realized he wanted an answer he smacked her again and began to rip off her clothing. "You've been fucking, and I can smell it on you and you're cheating on me huh?" When he pulled Diana to her feet with her clothes off and crying Amar turning her around to face him. Amar saw the bruises on her buttocks and hips and blanked out hitting her, Diana passed out.

North Carolina

Things seem to work themselves out for Lindsay because her shift was different when Lindsay returned to work. The Officers rotated four days on three days off the whole shift seemed weird miss Watkins was moved to another rotation and replaced by this middle-age white man who Lindsay never saw before. MS Watkins was harassed and asked to go through the metal detectors several times while going through her search to start the shift. MS Watkins was upset like she was the perfect officer but obviously her shit was catching up to her. When they all separated, she had the nerve to give Lindsay a foul look like she had something to do with her being moved off, the unit and placed in another area of the prison. Once they got to the dorm the white officer Mr. Blot was super strict and Petty. Officer Blot was strictly by the book you can hear a rat piss on cotton when He entered the prison unit. Lindsay saw the looks the Inmates gave when he came around the atmosphere was different.

Officer Blot made sure that Lindsay performed her job to the (T) that she made rounds every 30 minutes on the dot, he was a trip and when it was time for cell searches, they must have searched one man's cell for at least an hour. Lindsay sat back outside the cell door while Officer Blot went through every letter this man had every envelope every crack and crevice Lindsay saw the frustration of the inmate all over his face, even Lindsay knew that this search was extensive and extra. Officer Blot is what someone would call eccentric. Super cop, Officer Blot was probably picked on in high school as a youth and now exerts his power every chance he gets and uses his uniform to get away with it. While he was still tearing through the inmate's cell and ripping stuff up Lindsay looked around the block some inmates were watching TV or playing (spades) cards or playing chess and she saw this young man who just caught her attention, everything about him was different she has saw him before, but it was like his energy, made him stand out. His head was down at the table directly in front of her about 20 feet away he was reading or studying like she always saw him doing.

Lindsay saw the deep waves in his hair, the complexion of his skin, the way his fingers moved fluently when he wrote. The young man looked up and she looked away her heart beating out of her chest. "God who is this man" she thought, Lindsay immediately got butterflies in her stomach. Lindsay became self-conscious and started straightening her hair and looking for lent on her clothes anything to avoid his eyes he was back head down in his book. Lindsay couldn't help wondering what he was reading and most of all where this feeling was coming from. Who was or is this man? who has her for one nervous to look at him in his eyes? and for two thinking about who he is,?

and secretly feeling moisture in her love box that has never ever happened before.

"Officer" officer Blot repeated louder, Lindsay snapped out of her daze "You all, right?" Officer Blot asked and Lindsay now realizing that she had spaced out, heard Officer Blot "Un cuff him so I can strip search him" Officer Blot didn't have to but wanted to humiliate him. "Damn Blot, you already tore my cell up now you want to look at my ass too?" The inmate was furious, "You know the rules and procedures now put your clothes threw the trap." Officer Blot ordered. Lindsay Stood to the side, she wasn't allowed to observe the actual strip search "All right bend over, now squat and cough !!! squat down some more and cough." Blot commanded "I'm squatting Man damn." The inmate was hot and upset about the whole situation and truthfully Lindsay could empathize with him. Officer Blot was extra for no reason. When they finished something else happened, that changed everything the young man looked up from his reading and he and Lindsay made eye contact for the first time.

And for both, it seemed like the entire world stopped and moved in slow motion no words were ever exchanged but everything was said. their souls had spoken from that day and time Nothing would ever be the same. "Blot get your faggot Robo cop ass out of here" someone yelled from somewhere in the dorm Officer Blot's face turned blood red from embarrassment. Eventually Lindsay's position was rotated, and she went into the booth to control the doors inside the control booth her thoughts were racing 'why can't I stop thinking about him? I don't even know his name, where he is from, what am I thinking he's locked up, but what if he's about to be released'. All kinds of thoughts were running through Lindsay 's mind some even shocked her. That night when she got home, she took a hot shower and washed her body and for the very first time she explored her own body. It was as if her fingers had a mind of their own. Lindsay laid on her back and closed her eyes and all she could see was this mysterious man's eyes, his waves and skin complexion. And her fingers danced from her chocolate nipples teasing and pinching them to rubbing her stomach and down to her thighs until she couldn't take it any longer, her breathing began to speed up and Lindsay was rubbing her clitoris, For the first time. The sensation took her breath away as she experienced her first orgasm ever.

In his cell Charles couldn't get comfortable it was like the pillow wouldn't sit right no matter which way he turned he couldn't rest or get comfortable, so he dealt with the obvious. Thinking to himself 'Who is this CO (Correctional Officer) so beautiful with her chocolate sun kissed complexion, A queen who couldn't stop staring at him' Charles was not conceded nor vulgar towards women his mother taught him better than that, but he saw all the signs This Miss.... Miss Jones yes that was her name. God she was amazing 'But I don't have time for this I have a life sentence what would she want with me?' He thought she didn't seem to move like Miss Watkins or some of the other CO's that prayed on the lifers, having husbands and baby father 's at home but coming into the prison flirting and leading thirsty deprive prisoners on. Charles fought his thoughts all night long and still couldn't get any sleep all he saw when he closed his eyes was Miss Jones thank God her shift would be off for a few days so he could continue to work on his case because truthfully, he didn't need any distractions his goal was to declare his innocence and get out of prison. Maybe it was all in his head 'She probably was just staring at me because I look familiar yeah that's probably what it is' was his last thought before finally dozing off.

Dallas Texas

"Now if you will turn to the book of Acts   chapter 5" The Pastor read verse one "But a certain man name Ananias with sapphire his wife sold a possession and kept he back part of the proceeds. His wife also being aware of it and brought a certain part and laid it at the apostles' feet. Verse 3" The Pastor of the church Bishop Jakes spoke to the stadium packed crowd in his Mega Church. And he's making sure that everyone in attendance hears his sermon. The stadium was filled of over

100,000 guests in Dallas Texas. This was a three-day revival many people came in singing along to live performances by Donnie McClurkin, CeCe Winan's and Kirk Franklin the place was packed, and this was the closing day Peter was holding Dr. Bradford 's hand while she was in awe with the way Bishop Jakes preached the word of God on the stage. He was even being displayed on an overhead projector just like sports games you can see the sweat building on his face as he marched and yelled into his headset ushers would have to pick certain women up because they were passing out "But Peter... said Ananias why has Satan filled your heart to lie to the Holy Spirit and keep back part of the price of the land for yourself?" He spoke to the crowd "See some of you are holding back yes you are". Many people repeated with him throughout the crowd "You have it to give but you hold back thinking you're going to miss out !! that you're going to be without; But you're just like Ananias yes you.!! are you going to continue to doubt? He continues to read. "While it remained was it not your own? And after it was sold; was it not your own control? Why have you conceived this thing in your heart? in each of you all to do what is natural and after it was revealed. So why is it not your own control why can you not see that Satan has placed this thing in your heart you have not lied to Man but God to God's people not me." The Pastor shouted, "Not your love ones but God stop it stop it stop it stop lying to God and stop stealing

from the treasure chest in heaven stop stealing from yourself"
He wiped his forehead and the choir started singing and the
collection plates were passed around and some people got up
to go to one of the ATM machines in the church to make
another withdrawal to put in the collection plate. Several
people were called up specifically to come get healing and then
anyone was allowed DR Bradford looked at Peter and Peter
walked with her to the front. Oil was placed on both their
heads in the sign of the cross. Dr. Bradford was so happy she
couldn't stop smiling Peter and Dr. Bradford went to dinner
that evening and Peter talked and discussed life plans, and the
wedding which was in a few weeks. Peter was dressed
comfortably in a short shearling that stopped at the waist.
navy blue with white fur, polo shirt and pants and sneakers by
coach 1941 he had on his Frederique constant watch "Peter
you are an amazing man and have accomplished so much I
want to thank you so much for keeping your word and
attending this revival with me." Dr. Bradford was looking
Peter in his eyes spilling her heart out because she had wanted
to attend this revival for years and now, she had the chance to
enjoy it with her future son-in-law "Thank you so much I owe
you Peter" Dr Bradford said licking her lips and sipping her
wine. "Mrs. Bradford it was my pleasure" Peter assured her.
"Please call me Yvonne darling" Peter saw where Shaniqua got
her green eyes and honey complexion from her mother. Mrs.

Bradford was gorgeous older but well-kept "I wish Dr. Bradford could have attended with us." Peter stated", Mrs. Bradford sucked her teeth "Dennis has lost his spirit when we first met, he would have flown me to the Moon on his back, but things have changed again thank you Peter thank you so much." "Your welcome Mrs. Bradford" "Yvonne Peter!" Dr Bradford reached her manicure hands across the table and gently squeezed Peters hand and they both smiled. "Peter, I believe it's time to go" Together they arrive back at the hotel and Peter always the gentleman helped her out of the vehicle and together they rode the elevator to her suite in the elevator she removed her shoes and hugged Peter closely. Peter walked her up to her room "Good evening, Yvonne I'll be up early so we can prepare for our flights tomorrow." Peter stated but Dr. Bradford squeezed in tight and said softly "Peter please stay for a little while please and then you can go down to your room" Peter agreed to stay. The Suite was beautiful full queen size bed, champagne on ice "Peter sit down get comfortable baby" Dr Bradford went into the bathroom and Peter removed his coat and tried to relax a little. About 15 minutes later Dr. Bradford came out of the bathroom dressed provocatively in a peach Teddy that left nothing to the imagination she sashayed across the room and stood directly in front of Peter who looked like he seen a ghost "Peter darling relax" Dr Bradford said while rubbing his chest and kissing his lips Peter was in shock and stiff, frozen unable to move. Yvonne stuck her tongue in his ear and kissed his face and then she unbuckled his pants and put his penis in her mouth but no matter what Peter would not get an erection. Several moments later Dr. Bradford ran to the bathroom covering her face and in tears. Peter was shocked and confused he felt sad, Peter sat there in silence and at a lost for words seemed to last forever and then Peter straightened himself up and being a gentleman lightly knocked on the bathroom door "Don't cry Mrs. I mean Yvonne it's all right" "Go away I'm so embarrassed God what have I done?" It hurt Peter to hear her in there crying her heart out. Dr Bradford felt ashamed knowing that Peter could hear her crying in the bathroom. Several hours later Peter felt the door open because he refused to leave and ended up sitting at the door and dosed off, it had been a long day. When he woke up Dr. Bradford was her old self back in control and she explained how her and Dennis had not had sex in years between work and everything it was taking a toll on her, she had never cheated on him or even considered it. But with Peter "You stirred up emotions I had long suppressed and blocked out, Peter please forgive me I couldn't control myself" Peter started to speak, Dr Bradford put a hand up stopping him "I'll do anything for us to keep this a secret I don't want to hurt my daughter." Peter assured Dr. Bradford that he wouldn't ever mention this night he gave her a hug and he went to his room. Peter fell asleep finally in all his clothes.

North Carolina

"If you look closely this is where the suspect Treymon Green fatally shot Michael Young the 22 year old victim was shot 17 times outside of the One Shot Pool Hall right down the street from club Divas on new Bern Avenue here in Raleigh North Carolina, There is shocking footage of the whole incident which was filmed by several camera phones and if you take a look the suspect is seen arguing with the victim outside then shots are fired. The victim is trying to escape, and the suspect stands over the victim and shoots him at least 11 more times, a tragedy to the community; But what is most disturbing are the statements made by the suspect Treymon Green while getting into the police car after surrendering to authorities" "Fuck that you know who I am? Suave I'm Suave I'll be out in no time I wish one of you would say something to the police kill your whole family" "He's also seen spitting towards the people videotaping the scene this is Tanya Harris reporting live from channel 11 eyewitness news" Treymon Green aka Suave killed a young man who was supposedly trying to play him in front of a female inside his uncle's pool Hall and the young man tried to apologize to Suave trying to persuade him to cool down.

Suave made a scene, told him to step outside and shot him 17 times in cold blood. Some witnesses say Michael Young didn't even know the girl he was accused of talking to. The victim was a student at NC State a sophomore and had a promising future the boy's mother was hysterical and had to be taken to the hospital from the devastation and pain of the incident. Suave was last seen smiling in the back of the police car.

Central Prison

"Miss Jones, can I have some paper and envelopes please?" "Lindsay was sitting at the desk when Charles approached, and she smiled "how many you need?" "Just a couple please" "What else you need? "Lindsay asked touching his fingers as she gave him the envelopes. Charles felt like he had a frog stuck in his throat he was so nervous "I'm good thanks" even Lindsay's heart was beating like crazy she wanted this man; everything about him. Made him stand out his voice, skin tone, his manners even the way he walked. Charles was her first crush because Lindsay had never felt like this before in her entire life. Lindsay had wrestled with the what If's? worrying and all that and she had made her mind up And decided that she would not fight her feelings anymore she had been watching him for weeks and learned his name was Charles Altidore, but she still hadn't been nosy enough to

Google him and find out his case and all of the details. Lindsay still wanted to respect his privacy. Lindsay made her rounds around the block. and stepped at the door of his cell. and smiled as always, he was reading some big thick paged book "Hey" "Oh what's up" "Cell search" Lindsay stated. Charles got ready to have his cell searched thinking 'Damn I hope they don't tear my shit up' but when he looked around Lindsay was by herself "No... no cell search I just wanted to check on you" Charles was shocked of how open and honest she was he could see the sincerity in her eyes. "Miss Jones thanks for checking on me I'm OK" "Where are you from?" Lindsay asks like they were in the streets "Oh where am I from? I'm for Raleigh North Carolina" Charles responds, "I'm from Kingwood Forest me and my mom live there" Lindsay told him knowing that the information she just disclosed with him is completely against the policy and inappropriate, Charles knew this as well and was confused and had the look on his face "Relax What school did you go to?" she asked him and reached down running her hand over his waves. Lindsay licked her lips admiring how he groomed himself "I went to Southeast" Charles answered "What me too" they went over school days and he said "I thought you looked familiar you are a famous Track Star Lindsay Jones wow" Lindsay felt blessed and blushed when he told her he remembered all her records but the reason she didn't remember him was because Charles was a Square who loved chemistry and biology and although he was an honor roll student he wasn't very popular. "Miss Jones what are you doing here? you should be in college training getting ready for the Olympics" Lindsay looked down and said, "My mother got sick, so I needed to be with her" Charles stood up and saw the pain in Lindsay 's eyes "I'm sorry that's brave of you wow is she all right now?" Charles asked with much concern "Yeah she's better" Lindsay and Charles had been talking for over 30 minutes so Charles knowing how things would look to the other inmates in the cellblock looked around and saw the stares and looks from the convicts and dayroom inmates, and Charles said in a whisper "Miss Jones look I don't want to seem rude but we can't do this like this I mean" Charles was nervous "What?" Lindsay caught on "So look write this number down" she replied, "What? You're your number?" Charles stuttered and knew he heard her wrong. "Hurry up silly 919-123-4567 call me any time." Before Lindsay can walk out Charles stopped her "Wait Lindsay , I mean Miss Jones we have to be careful I don't want you to lose your job look its Kool but we have to pretend to be other people, like you work somewhere else and live in another state the phone calls are monitored" Charles was talking real fast and he could spot an old coon or as convicts say 'it was a snitch all in his mouth' "Oh I get it well call me Linda and act like I live in Hawaii always wanted to live there Kool?" "cool" Lindsay went out the cell and walked away ignoring all the looks from the guys standing or sitting around watching her leave Charles cell.

Georgia

Amar was driving reckless threw Atlanta towards New Smyrna Georgia to be specific. Joy riding in his brand-new McLaren it was yellow with yellow & black interior he has spent over $1 million for the vehicle. Amar had been drinking earlier in the day Amar was drinking more often enjoying getting saucy. Amar was still upset with Diana about her missing in action episode a few months back. He had blackened one of her eyes and had no remorse about it. Amar felt like Diana deserved it. He provided for Diana, helped with the roof over her head and clothes on her back She was too do what she was told... Amar was riding around with a young girl from Decatur who was probably barely 18 years old, but he didn't care as he said, "Pussy was Pussy", she was giving him head while he drove the vehicle, but it got so good to him he had to pull over and let her do her thing. So, he was on the side of the road leaning back and enjoying himself when a flashlight knocks on the driver side window. Amar was as hard as a Cîroc bottle and trying to fix himself up and hide the open bottle of Hennessy. "Roll down the window and turn off the ignition Sir" The Georgia State Trooper demanded while shining his light in Amar's face, he could smell the alcohol on

Amar's breath it was reeking out of his pores. "Yes.... Yes Officer ...Hey man you're really tall" Amar says He and the young girl began giggling like children. "License and registration please" "Hold your horses it's right here" Amar says to the Trooper. "Slowly" he replies Pulling out his side arm, "Please don't shoot us officer" the girl says. Amar reaches for the glove compartment but fumbles around he looks pitiful searching for his license "Son sit still and listen real carefully sit up straight, place your hands on the wheel of the vehicle, Unlock the door and get out the vehicle with your hands where I can see them" The State Trooper was dead serious as serious as cancer, and he had his hand on his gun. Amar got out of the car, and he stumbled and started laughing and then crying the trooper placed Amar in handcuffs and sat him on the pavement on the side of the road. Almost 10 to 15 minutes later a backup car arrives together the troopers place cones on the road to direct the traffic. Amar was given a breathalyzer test his alcohol level was way above legal standard and he's arrested for DWI Driving While Intoxicated the young girl is hysterical and asked repeatedly to be able to call her mother, so the Troopers separated the two of them. They were taken and driven downtown in separate cars to the police station while Amar is being booked and fingerprinted the officers are clowning and joking on him, "Amar how are you going to run against the Eagles this Monday night and your so wasted you don't know where you are?" the laughter was loud, and everyone took shots "Pipe down ladies" the captain commented. "We have some serious allegations here" "Oh come on cap it's just a DWI he's rich he'll be out and on the field in no time" "Young man it was just a DWI before that 15-year-old child told us what happened tonight "The captain replicd. "Now get him processed correctly and put him in the cell". There was no more joking Amar was too drunk to understand but the officers were now upset some of them had children and daughters of their own. Amar was taken before the magistrate and charged with one count of DWI and one count of first degree rape and given a $500,000 secured bond when Amar heard the rape charges he became sober immediately, "Hey I ain't rape no one I didn't rape no freaking body get off me, get off me I need to speak to my attorney" Amar was stripped searched and processed and allowed one phone call, his team attorney for the Atlanta Falcons bonded him out. Amar was bombarded by Paparazzi and photographers when he was released early the next morning and all his business was on the front-page news. ESPN and SportsCenter played it day and night, immediately after there was a press conference and Amar was somewhat sober with a throbbing headache and had brought Diana with him for support the photographers took pictures of them entering the building which was the headquarters for the Atlanta Falcons owners and GM's "Have a seat Mr. Jackson, Amar Jackson do you understand the allegations made against you? This incident has come out at a crucial time in our season especially playing tonight and this Sunday.

Chapter 10

Now I'm not here to point fingers or condemn you but we have policy and procedures at this franchise and it is called upon me as general manager to inform you that you are currently suspended for the next four games without pay, and also your now on disciplinary probation if found guilty we will have to even consider keeping you as a member of this franchise if you have any questions, comments, or concerns please consult your attorney and good day". Amar was excused he walked out with his head down feeling embarrassed and ashamed of himself. Diana was by his side when he left the building and took that dreadful trip home. Amar 's first court date was 10 days away which gave him time to think. Diana was afraid to confront him about the rape charges knowing his temper for once Amar was his old self. The charming gentle man Diana had first met. Amar cooked, cleaned and was kind and gentle and attentive he said he had a special surprise planned for her and it had been several days now since he got out of jail, so the anticipation was wearing her down. Diana 's mother called she was worried about Diana she had read about them in the newspaper and saw her daughter holding Amar's hand walking towards a waiting vehicle "Diana how are you sweetheart?" Her mother asked there was so much concern in her voice "Yes mom I'm OK mom how did you get my telephone number?" Diana asked coldly "I had to get it from that guy I saw you with in the paper his lawyer I had to go through a lot to find you baby I miss you, your father and I both miss you. we are your family Diana, we love you. we love you to death sweetheart," Diana could hear her mother crying, but she had grown to shut out her feelings and Diana stated icily "Yeah mom whatever where was the love when you and dad cut me off? Whatever, Bye...Mom I got to go and please don't contact me anymore"

Diana disconnected the call it has almost been 2 years since she has spoken with her mother and she almost cried but sucked it up. Diana needed a fix this whole situation with Amar kept her from contacting her connect Black and scoring some more drugs "Diana come on let's ride" "Amar where we going? Baby it's 8 o'clock, let's stay home and just relax" Diana said in her Latin accent gently and meek. "Baby please I want to do what I should've done a long time ago" "Amar I need to get dressed give me some time at least 30 minutes" Diana didn't play that just looking any kind of way "OK but hurry up please" 45 minutes later Diana was dressed in a polyester dress viscose blend Turtleneck and a pair of studded suede Jimmy Choo knee-high boots along with her Furla leather bag. Amar was dressed in an all-black Armani suit when they stepped out of the house there was a stretched Escalade equipped with TVs and all the Luxuries waiting out front. They were driven to the airport and boarded a private jet, on the flight they ate and sipped champagne and sat back and enjoyed the ride, before they knew it, they were landing and Diana saw all the lights in the desert and knew immediately they were in Las Vegas "Amar what are we doing here?" Diana asked excited "It's a surprise" They were escorted to the hotel suite, On the walk through Diana noticed they were greeted by some shady stares Especially with Amar's current situation with all the press coverage involving him with rape charges and being a professional football player once in the suite Amar had a live violinist playing over a table made for two, It was very romantic., And waiters brought out food,. During the meal Amar got a one knee and proposed to Diana and presented a 3 1/2 carat diamond ring To Diana it fit perfect. Diana didn't know what to say, in that instance right before her eyes Diana saw all the times spent with Amar the good, bad and ugly, but Diana loved him. And wanted to trust him and now these last couple of days he made love to her and was so nice like the beginning and she really wanted to make things work and looking at his desperate eyes while on his knees she couldn't remember saying it, but it was said, and Amar jumped for joy and picked her up "When Amar Baby When baby?" Diana asked so she could prepare properly "Right Now" Amar responded. "Right now? are you serious?"

Diana was confused "Yes D right now" Amar left her standing there got on the phone and into the room came a few make-ups artist, cosmetologist and a Korean woman holding a white Theia Courtney Ombre strapless Bridal dress. Diana tried on the strapless dress with satin pedals the dress was beautiful, and it was her size to the tee. Amar was fitted in a Tuxedo and with Her mouth still wide two hours later in Las Vegas Nevada Amar and Diana got married and Diana was now Diana Jackson.

The next day Diana got up and questioned the bellhop on how to score some blow (cocaine) and 20 minutes later sitting on the toilet Diana locked the door and took a snort of cocaine and read the newspaper and what she saw totally blew her high, on the cover was a photo of Amar and Diana in the headlines in bold print Amar Jackson sneaks off to Las Vegas and has secret wedding to hide his pass infidelities , Diana dropped the paper. and continued to get high tears running down her face.

Central Prison

" You have a collect call from Charles Altidore from Central prison to accept this call press five to terminate this call please   hang up, Thank you this call is   subject to monitoring and recording"   "Hello" they both were still nervous and had been talking at least once a day especially since the prison system changed the policy and put four telephones in each block and reduced not only the phone rate but allowed individuals to make as many calls as they could afford. Lindsay knew she had to take control because Charles was Shy "Hey silly talk to me you miss me?" Lindsay asked giggling like a schoolchild "Yes, I do... I did, I mean do, you know what I'm saying" Charles had butterflies in his stomach Lindsay had brought out a side of him that he had to hide for years. She made him smile and laugh and most importantly made him feel alive again. For so long Charles has been in prison and focus solely on his day in court to prove his innocence that he had no time for anything else and Lindsay was his angel she had given him a new outlook on life a new drive a new purpose still it was always that nagging voice "You got life she don't want you" He tried to ignore it And just focus on the here and now "Did you get my present?" "Yes, thank you I can't thank you enough that means so much to me". Lindsay had sent Charles $100 Jay Pay and a Christmas card not because he asked but because she wanted to, he didn't even know it was coming.

Last Wednesday Lindsay worked his unit and she noticed how Charles never went to canteen his sneakers were worn down and they were old, still she knew it was something different about Charles he was special call it women's intuition Lindsay had a soft spot for Charles and only had eyes for him shoot Lindsay could spot Charles in a million Man march, Lindsay was concerned about Charles in the facility and wanted to make sure that he ate well, even MS Joanne said that Lindsay had been bit by the love bug. Lindsay had a new walk and was giddy and glowing all the time, Lindsay was happy especially when she had to work in Charles block.

Charles and Lindsay, they would talk sometimes pass notes because he would tape a note or poem to the back of his ID card and then go to the desk where Lindsay was stationed and request a newspaper or toilet tissue and she would take his ID card and secretly remove the note and tape, and no one would be the wiser. So, on her bathroom breaks or lunch break she would read it "I opened a PO Box so you can write me whenever you want" Lindsay said, and Charles could hear her smile and feel her joy over the phone. "You think that's safe?" "Don't worry silly it's in a friends name." Truthfully, it was in Big Mamas name she wouldn't mind Lindsay learned that Charles no matter what always thought about her safety and well-being "OK because I like writing you" "You do? what else you like?" "Lindsay could feel herself getting moist sitting on her bed on the phone with Charles. "Well, your eyes the way they shine and sparkle like to diamonds in the snow and God your um... you know" "No I don't tell me" Lindsay said boldly and in a sexy tone. Charles was so gentle and respectful he couldn't say it "Your, you know? you know what I'm trying to say... you know what I want to say?" He laughed so hard in his nervousness "My ass is that what you're talking about?" Lindsay said and Charles eyes popped out his head. "Yes, it is really nice and looks soft." "Charles" Lindsay said his name slow as she touched herself. In a real slow and low tone she said "I'm going to let you feel it" "Oh no no I can't I wouldn't I wouldn't do that" "You have 60 seconds remaining" the operator interrupted "Call me back" Lindsay shouted "you sure" "Yes I'm sure peanut head I want to talk to you" Lindsay had never had a boyfriend and Charles brought out the side of her that sometimes shocked her she wanted this man his smell, yes his scent was a turn on for Lindsay she could remember his hand writing, the words he used in his letters he was a lot bolder.

In person he was coy nothing sexual or inappropriate just more confident but that was different. Now face-to-face over the phone he was a scaredy-cat. Lindsay loved to call him names she called him all kinds of names, but he never got angry he was so cool. When Charles called back, they talked some more Lindsay quizzed him about her birthday or her favorite color or favorite ice cream to see if he remembered she felt good he remembered everything "I'm going to a wedding in two weeks."

Lindsay told him "Oh that's cool where" "In New York one of my best friends is getting married and I'm the maid of honor" "I wish I could be there with you" Charles sounded down "Me too" Lindsay replied they both were silent for a moment thinking how that would be a dream come true for them to be together comfortable outside of the prison and free. "Have fun and please try to catch the bouquet of flowers the bride throws I heard its good luck." Charles said with a little bass in his voice "Why not? It might. Be our wedding next" Charles couldn't respond "Anyway I'll send you photos don't worry I know what you're thinking, and I got this." Charles was thinking about her safety and Job he didn't want Lindsay to take a photo of herself because someone in the mail room may notice and rat her out "Have you done this before?" Charles Asked sarcastically "No silly I just have to take care of you God told me I'm your angel" Charles had tears in his eyes he was just starting to question God wondering why he was placed in such an unjust and hostile predicament for something he didn't really do. Lindsay hadn't even asked him why he was locked up and he figured he would wait until she asked and then he would open up and tell her his story they both hung up feeling that bittersweet feeling both looking forward to the next time that they saw one another.

New York

It was a beautiful Valentine's Day, although it had snowed the day before; Today wasn't cold. The temperature was nice, and of course, it was snow all over, making the day picture-perfect for Shaniqua. She looked out the window as her mother straightened her dress looking into a full-length mirror Shaniqua turned around in a full circle "Lindsay how do I look?" "Amazing" and she did Diana was coming but she hadn't showed up yet there was still time "I always dreamed of this the day God I'm so happy" "This is your day sweetie, and you deserve Peter he's a good man" Dr. Bradford said almost choking and starting to cough "Mom please get a water you're scaring me." Diana came in wide eyed and happy "Hey look at you" Diana was loud as usual, and she brought a gift and gave it to Shaniqua giving both her and Lindsay long hugs and the gang was back together. "Oh, Shaniqua God you look gorgeous" "Thank you I'm so nervous" "Don't be it's easy like eating cake" "Yeah that's easy for you to say we heard about you Miss Jackson" Lindsay and Shaniqua said at the same time. Diana began blushing and covered her face showing off her diamond ring. "God that's nice" Lindsay found herself a little jealous they were both married to skilled professional strong Black men she thought to herself 'It's not about me today. Today is about Shaniqua' Diana lowered her voice conspiratorially "I'll fill you in later of all the details" the girls giggled and did their ritual of locking pinkies.

All the women wore white or off-white or eggshell or even cream. They made it to Times Square on time. Peter was dressed to the 9's and all his brothers were in attendance. Peters father was looking dapper in his older patriarchal way and of course Peters mother who wouldn't smile if someone had placed a baby in her hands was there. Shaniqua paid her no mind, Shaniqua 's mother and father was also seated in the front row on the other side of Peters family.

A few of Shaniqua 's cousins were there one kept giving Diana the evil eye on the low because Diana and her famous football playing husband Amar Jackson was in attendance, Amar was a whole other story with the cameras he seem to create a whole new situation wherever he went and 'Earth to Diana didn't she tell him it was an all-white affair' Lindsay thought to herself. Tuxedos for men or cream off-white this man had on a rainbow colored Coogie sweater and matching pants, platinum necklace with a diamond encrusted football pendant that was blinding everyone and a diamond bezel Cartier watch. When Shaniqua saw Amar, she agreed he was handsome but conceded was not the word. Amar also pulled up in a Bugatti when everyone else came together in limousines.

The time square church was huge and at the moment Shaniqua walked down the aisle everything was perfect. The Pastor read from the bible then Peter and Shaniqua's said their vowels they confirmed the vowels before family and friends and all those in attendance. "I now with the power vested in me I now Pronounce you husband and wife." Everyone was clapping and taking pictures as they kissed and then Shaniqua turned around to throw the flower bouquet overhead and it seem to sail through the air in slow motion. Lindsay was telling one of the flower girls who was maybe only seven or eight years old about the two newlyweds kissing "I don't kiss boys" the young girl was saying with her face turnt up "Yes I know but watch out!!" Lindsay could tell the girl was focused on something, and she turned just in time as a reflex to really block her face. She caught the bouquet of flowers, and everyone started clapping and hollering. Diana looked at Lindsay and Mouthed "Your next?" Lindsay was stunned and just smiled and shook her head thinking about Charles. Shaniqua and Peter ran out of the church after they jumped the broom two children were holding and to Shaniqua's delight Peter told her to look up and, on the Times, Square display screen was both Peter and Shaniqua's picture in live view in real time Looking wonderful and happy both Peter and Shaniqua smiled and kissed again. Greg was in the background, but he seemed distant and here comes Mr. Amar Jackson with sunglasses on to get right in front of the bride and groom and wave 'No he didn't' Lindsay thought. Peter and Shaniqua maneuvered around him and was driven away by

164

horse and carriage by two Beautiful Arabian White horses to the reception location. They had rented the ballroom in the Ritz Carlton. It was splendid. Triple layer cakes the bride shoes were boxed up as souvenirs or to remember this day Brian McKnight followed by Mary J Blige sang for the guest. There was a soul train line and people showed out kids ran around with sparklers there was wine, bottles of Ace of Spades food from all over even a dish of Zanzibar coconut fish, curry fried chicken, Macaroni and cheese, sweet potato pies, you name it and it was there. "Shaniqua girl I did not know your father could dance" Diana said Clowning "He can't I don't know what in the world has gotten into him and what he was thinking he was just doing" "You should have seen the expression on his face" Lindsay laughed. They all laughed "Diana why is my cousin looking at you like you killed his dog" Shaniqua asked. "He'll get over it" Diana said and began filling the girls in about living in Atlanta and getting married in Vegas. Of course, Diana never mentioned about Amar being abusive she kept that part to herself "Diana isn't that Amar all up in that white girl face?" Shaniqua pointed Lindsay looked "Yes what the hell did he just kiss her?" both of them looked at Diana and then when they saw her expression it seemed as if she was as cool as a cucumber about the whole thing they really tripped "Girl I know that is not your man? I mean excuse me your husband kissing some white woman or any other woman for that matter at my wedding disrespecting us and especially you?" Shaniqua was livid and got up and Diana got up and grabbed her arm and sat her back down "Chill chill please !!" Diana pleaded, "What are you crazy?" "Calm down , look me and Amar have an understanding" "Understanding" both Lindsay and Shaniqua said at the same time "He should be under the table while we standing over him kicking his ass" Shaniqua said , Shaniqua had changed a lot because here she was cursing like a sailor again "look y'all it is cool we have an open relationship hell it's 2015 everyone's into it and she is kind of cute" Diana said "Oh hell no girl have you bumped your head too many times she's what?" Shaniqua was blown away. Lindsay intervened "let it go if that's how they get down and Diana and him are happy and safe cool" Lindsay said trying to diffuse the situation. Shaniqua just shook her head just then a group of seven men dressed in firemen uniforms ran into the room the DJ stopped the music and everyone automatically started looking around like 'what's going on?' one of the men said "We heard there's a fire in here and we're here to put it out" immediately the music changed and came back on and the men began to remove their clothes each of them was cut up and looked chiseled by god's hands himself. The women went crazy the men crowded around the bride Shaniqua was shocked and caught completely off guard. One guy was now completely nude they were hired by Diana from

Chip & Dales. They gyrated on Shaniqua and on all the women some of the kids sat with their mouths open Peter didn't seem to mind but Dr. Bradford was looking livid, and MS Bradford was in a trance. Lindsay was lost for words Diana was being carried around by one of the firemen and bouncing on his lap "Enough Enough out out out out out" Shaniqua's father blanked on the DJ "Stop the music" after the episode they were escorted out and things returned somewhat to normal Shaniqua's father was still sweating and upset with whomever turned his daughter's wedding into a circus. Diana sat with Amar and his latest conquest an Italian woman who worked with the catering company for the weeding. They all agreed to hook up later for some fun "Lindsay come here let me introduce you to Michael" "Hey Michael" "Hey sis how you are feeling" Micheal gave Shaniqua a hug and kiss on the cheek and congratulated her again "Yes you are officially my brother now this is Lindsay and she's single and my best friend so you better not hurt her" Shaniqua stated before leaving them alone. Lindsay looked like a deer Caught in a truck's headlights "Hello it's a pleasure to meet you" Michael said holding out his hand Lindsay excepted it his hand was warm he was handsome charming and just the right height "I'm going to leave you two alone" Shaniqua left to go find Peter who she spotted talking to Greg. Lindsay and Michael hit it off good he kept Lindsay laughing and smiling and he wasn't too forceful but no matter what he said or how good he looked he wasn't Charles and even being in New York far away from Raleigh for the first time she felt like somehow she was betraying Charles and felt terrible about it just then her phone rang " You have a collect call from" Before the operator could finish Lindsay had press all the buttons she knew them now by heart. It felt so good when Charles said hello. Lindsay held her finger up to Michael to signal that the call was important and turned her back to him to find a quiet Place to talk "Charles I miss you and I love you" "Wow I miss you too and that's what I'll called to tell you I love you too" "They talked for 4 phone calls back to back, Charles even ignored the stares from certain inmates who were mean mugging him, because he had repeatedly used the phone back to back. After the call Michael tried to resume where he left off, but it was hard pressed and awkward. Lindsay 's mind and heart was somewhere else Micheal got the picture and stepped off not rude but respectfully as a gentleman Lindsay took his business card to be polite and not hurt his ego, he was a gentleman but again he wasn't Charles.

Shaniqua and Peter snuck out and rode to the airport and they flew to the Canary Islands and it was beautiful the islands are located south east of Morocco and this time of year the weather was hot and majestic so it was all like a fairytale to Shaniqua they had a romantic setting a bungalow with satin white drapes around a canopy bed blowing from the ocean breeze Peter laid Shaniqua down and kiss every inch of her body massaged her skin rubbing oil all over her from head to toe. He kissed up her stomach to her areolas and sensitive nipples until she begged to be penetrated, he slowly Trailed kisses back down her stomach and then slowly to her clitoris. Shaniqua had orgasm after orgasm she was still a virgin so this was her first orgasm and words couldn't describe the feeling she felt she stopped Peter pulled him up and kissed his lips tasting her our own juices and pushed him on his back "Peter I love you" she kissed his chest And suck on his flaccid member but no matter what he wouldn't get an erection Shaniqua kept trying pulling on it everything but nothing.... she was confused and she looked at him like 'Help me, what should I do?' Peter took over laid her back and slid his fingers into her with his thumb circling her clitoris and penetrated her with his fingers. Shaniqua was now relaxing and eventually grinding on his fingers and began fucking his hand and that was how Shaniqua lost her virginity by Peters hand.

CHAPTER 11

Raleigh NC

Lindsay had a few days off and was just chilling around the house she was grateful that Shaniqua had given her a year-to-date Lincoln MKZ this was Lindsays first vehicle she was so excited she had taken Big Mama and her mother Miss Joanne for a drive and Big Mama liked being out the house but eventually she wanted to go back home she said that her back and feet were hurting. Lindsay could see her ankles were swollen and toes hurt in her shoes. "Nana I know how much you love sweets but the doctor says you need to slow down" "I know child but it's hard" Big mama had looked like she was in a lot of pain lately and Lindsay blamed it all on her eating habits especially pork she cooked it all the time even used lard for grease, Most Black people didn't know or didn't realize that when you eat pork it didn't take an immediate toll on your body or have instant effects it hurt your body in the long run over a long period of time , like sugar with years and years of consumption had a detrimental effect on your health. Lindsay was excited when she heard that Charles received the photos of the wedding. Charles had never been out of North Carolina and wanted to travel Lindsay assured him that one day he would, that they would, and he tried to sound hopeful and enthusiastic about it, but he was serving a life sentence.

Lindsay still hadn't asked Charles how much time he had or why he was even locked up in prison. She just couldn't bring herself to look him up she felt like that was invading his privacy, and she just wanted to put everything in god's hands Lindsay wasn't a Bible thumper she still prayed the best way she knew how, and Charles made her feel good. Lindsay wasn't concerned with his time she just hoped he would be out soon later that evening the phone rang and she was hoping it was Charles when she picked up the phone but it was Shaniqua "Well hello to You too... acting all stank" "Oh no it's not like that Shaniqua don't act like that, I just thought you were someone else that's all" Lindsay said "Who? Michael how did things go between you two? I told you he was handsome and paid girl he's perfect, isn't he?" "Well, um... He's OK he's very respectful, handsome and we did speak about his career but" Lindsay found herself stuck because all that Michael was, he still wasn't Charles. "He and I have someone already" Lindsay said when she said it, she wanted to take it back "You what? hell, knaw why didn't you say something, why didn't you bring him to my wedding? come on Lindsay were best friends we always said we wouldn't keep secrets" Shaniqua sounded hurt, and Lindsay wished she would have kept her big mouth shut "No I'm not keeping secrets I was just waiting for the right time, and you know with the wedding and everything.... I just kept it to myself plus we've been just talking for a few months" Lindsay was sweating now "Months and I'm just hearing about him okay scratch that please fill me in, and I want all the details". Lindsay was at a loss for words and suddenly, her mouth was dry "Alright his name is Charles he's from Raleigh like us" Lindsay said excitedly "Do I know him? what school did he go to?" Shaniqua was eager to know. "Slow down slow down" Lindsay tried her best to describe Charles without stepping on a land mine and she was close but no cigar "So when can I meet him, he sounds like a great guy and when I come to Raleigh we can go out" Shaniqua planned "Kool I know Charles would love to meet you" Lindsay said nervously. Lindsay felt terrible as soon as the words came out. Hell, how could Shaniqua meet Charles he was locked up they couldn't even talk on the phone unless he called, and she was there to accept his call gosh she was in a bind. "So enough about me how was your honeymoon" Lindsay asked to try to clear the conversation and steer things in another direction "Lindsay it was beautiful the Canary Islands the crystal-clear waters. OH... It was amazing the fruits and foods" "So now you're officially a woman" Lindsay says with a bit of envy because now she was the only virgin in the crew. Shaniqua felt self-conscious because she wasn't sure if technically, she was still a virgin of course with peters situation he never penetrated her and although she tried the next day to seduce and make love to Peter, he claimed to be under a lot of stress and strain. so she acted as a good wife and gave her husband space, they agreed to relax and enjoy the peace and tranquility outside of the hustle and bustle of New York City "Yes I am and I feel different, I feel complete now that I found my soulmate my other half but girl you know what?" "What? "Lindsay replied "I can't believe Diana has lost it and I didn't know she was you know?" "Lesbian or bisexual rather" "Yes and that Amar is completely disrespectful, and my father is still pissed about those strippers" Shaniqua added "You got to admit that was crazy". They both laughed but Shaniqua got serious "Lindsay Diana never even mentioned about Amar's allegations of raping a young girl found in his car that night of his arrest" Shaniqua added "I saw that" "I just didn't want to bring it up because it was my wedding day and also I kind of felt bad but for her to play it off like it was nothing and on top of that she married him truthfully I don't think I know Diane anymore" Lindsay had to agree things were different and the girls seem to be growing apart somewhat, just taking on their own identity and life. "Now let's not give up on her she still our friend" Lindsay said with love in her voice "Yeah you're right so have you been driving your car?" "Yes, thank you so much" "Now you and Charles can do the nasty in the car" Shaniqua said in a low voice making Lindsay squirm in panic "Well I love you Lindsay call me anytime OK" "OK love you too bye".

'Wow what have I gotten myself into?' Lindsay thought to herself Lindsay never lied but this one time she felt compelled to defend Charles, but she knew the saying was true as the saying goes once you tell one lie you got to tell another one.

Atlanta

Diana ran to the bathroom and almost missed the toilet vomiting again she has thrown up every morning for the last two days. "Baby what's up? you alright?" Amar asked while bending down and rubbing her back Diana plays it off "Yeah must be something I ate". "I'm going to fix you a glass of ginger ale clean yourself up" Amar went to the kitchen and Diana washes her face and brushes her teeth. Diana feels a little bit better she's really just a little crabby because Amar is always up early and he's nosy so nosy that she can't take her last bump of heroin she still has that she scored from Black recently "Diana girl come on" "I'm coming" ' damn' "Diana thinks trying to get her hair fixed she thinks to herself 'I can't wait till he gets back to playing football he's like a big kid sitting around the house eating cereal playing video games all day' Amar is to meet with his attorney Thursday because there was a scheduled hearing Friday on his charges. From what she knew about the whole situation Amar's Attorney was trying to keep the whole case out of the tabloids away from the media he was pushing to pay off the young girl and her family but before all of that, Amar had to appear in court "Diana" "what?" Diana shouted coming out the bathroom into the master bedroom and Amar was nude his muscular frame sitting up on his knees facing her with his manhood in his hands erect. "Why so cranky Mamacita come to daddy I'll fix it" Amar said in a soothing voice seconds later Diana was moaning because of the grip Amar had on both her ass cheeks with his tongue doing magic one her clitoris just as Diana had an orgasm he flipped her over doggy style and began to taste her juices from the back "Amar Que Rico Pappi" Amar used his tongue every way to take Diana to the heavens then he fills her completely with his young strong wood. If they had neighbors, they would hear Diana and may have thought she needed help the way Amar was pounding inside her. Diana lost count of how many orgasms she had, and Amar was still going, sweating, and talking to Diana smacking her on the Ass. "This is my pussy? answer me."

Diana was worn out and fell asleep. When she woke up, she fixed herself up because she refused to leave the house looking like anything or thrown away. Diana tipped toed out of the house because Amar was sleep and she did not want to wake him or his wood up again. God that young man is a beast, and his tongue can spell open sesame in any language. Diana thought to herself when she got into the car the very first thing

Diana did was look for her drugs. lately her habit has begun to increase when she first started, she would do a bag or two a day now she was doing 10 or 15 bags just to knock the feeling off and get her day started. Diana drove to the drugstore to pick up a pregnancy test. Her period Hadn't showed up in a couple of weeks Diana figured that the morning sickness was from the drugs. But her morning sickness as of lately was different. Diana didn't want to drive home with the test, so she went to a public bathroom urinated on the stick and let it sit on the sink anxiously waiting and sure enough she was pregnant. "No No No this can't be right" she panicked and opened the other box she brought to take another test. squatted and made herself urinate again and sat down and waited frustrated. Diana didn't want to be a mother she was too young she had dropped out of school Amar was to controlling. Shit who was she fooling? not herself. Amar was abusive and the worst part was Diana didn't know who the baby's father was. Diana cried as she thought about her life and how she was raped and violated by those men at the party. Alexis had tricked her into attending. Diana remembered vividly that no one used protection when they used and penetrated her body. And now she sat on the toilet feeling defeated even the second pregnancy test showed positive she cried wishing she had someone to talk to.

New York

Shaniqua was having a cappuccino in her kitchen when Peter strolls in Peter is dressed in a cashmere and silk sweater and cotton chino slacks by Ralph Lauren and suede sneakers by strange Matter "Good morning honey" Peter kisses Shaniqua. And she is delighted by his affection. Things have been great around the house they are coexisting quite well getting along. Shaniqua's still on a mission to be the best Defensive attorney in the state and she has since been taking on more cases. "Congratulations on that Krause case you are amazing" "Thank you Peter it was obviously an illegal search and seizure so therefore the officers and detectives overstepped their authority, and I showed the jury their negligence." "Indeed, that you did miss Johnson" "I love it when you say that, Peter!!! my new name" Shaniqua smiled and looked into Peters eyes. Shaniqua was deeply in love with Peter he was the center of her universe. "Peter let's have dinner tonight" "Not tonight sweetheart Thursday I'm free tonight Greg and I have some important paperwork to go over" "All right Thursday is good I'm off." Shaniqua left the home and headed to her office to tackle the obstacles of the day in the life of law and order.

Atlanta

Several weeks later Diana was in her OBGYN 's office feeling nauseous and embarrassed because she was going to terminate her pregnancy and she looked around at the other women they're thinking to herself 'Everyone knows she was a murderer' a cold-hearted killer because that's what it boils down to in her mind that child living in her womb is innocent 'But what about me? God Amar will flip if it's a healthy baby and all but what if it's not his? how could I explain that? and then what do I do? where do I live? me and my baby when he puts me out?' So many thoughts were running through Diana's mind. "Miss Jackson, Miss Jackson the Doctor is available to see you" Even Diana was looking around as the nurse repeated herself then it dawned on Diana, she was no longer Diana Lopez but now Jackson. "Oh gosh I am here I'm sorry". Diana seemed honest and innocent, but the nurse wasn't buying it she looked a Diana like spoiled food. Although Diana was dressed in a Ralph Lauren cashmere turtleneck and fatigue cargo pants and Max Mara acetate and metal sunglasses with her hands gripping tightly on her Salvatore Ferragamo handbag the nurse could see right through her, Diana stood right outside the door of the Doctors office, Diana, and the nurse were never very close one day in the past turned their relationship sour. Diana had been coming here since she moved to Atlanta from California and Dr. Richardson was a big flirt and the Nurse felt some type away since Diana had come and started receiving all the looks and attention from Dr. Richardson. After the nurse did the prepping and the signing of Paperwork in came Dr. Richardson "Oh how's my favorite patient Miss Lopez Oh excuse me Mrs. Jackson." Dr. Richardson looked like Ice-T the actor and music artist and he was highly intelligent and sexy which was a Deadly combination, but Diana had kept it strictly business and never fed into his advances or suggestions of an affair. "Yes, I am married now" Dr. Richardson looked at the ring on her finger and said "I see, and Amar Jackson is a very popular man especially with the ladies I hear" Diana caught on to his sarcasm and tried not to let her emotions show. But she was the failing. Amar was young and reckless, and his business was all over and not just Atlanta or the national football league but everywhere. Diana had to pay that price to although she was discreet with hers. "Miss Jackson, I want to go over some things now it's your right by the state of Georgia to terminate the pregnancy but there are some things and concerns I must go over with you, OK?" Diana nodded her head. "Nancy, could you step out please" The nurse was looking livid like there was no reason for her to have to leave, "Yes no problem" she said sarcastically. "Now tell me how Mr. Jackson feels about the procedure?" "What?" Diana was upset and sat up in her chair. "Look that is none of your concern this is a private matter concerning only me it's about me" Diana stated boldly. "Calm down, calm down no need to get upset all I'm saying is there's nosy vindictive money hungry people out there in this world Miss Jackson that would love to find out that the newlywed of Athlete Amar Jackson accused I don't want to sound too harsh, but rapist Amar Jackson has recently terminated her pregnancy". Diana was blown away 'This snake in the grass'. "And how would they find that out? when we have a confidential clause?" "Yes, we do but things happen, but to ensure your safety... because all I want is to keep you safe, I'm thinking we can work things out." Dr. Richardson whispered while stroking himself, looking Diana in the eyes. 'How do I always end up in these situations with these freaking creeps' Diana thought to herself. "Dr. Richardson what your suggestion is blackmail, and, in my mind, I really want to call my lawyer and sue your ass for everything you got" Diana spoke with authority to show that she wasn't a pushover. Dr Richardson got up slowly and walked over to his desk and picked up his cell phone and a plastic cylinder cup with a red top on it. "Here be my guest but before you call your lawyer remembered that we took your blood and urine samples, and you tested positive for both cocaine and heroin now I'm sure your husband is not going to like the fact that his wife who is pregnant! probably highly addicted to opioids is in my office planning to terminate the fetus without his knowledge and this story also will make front page news and become the talk of the football community in a whole" Diana began to cry "Oh now now just be a nice girl and play nice" "What do you want?" "Dr. Richardson walked to the door and locked it removed his white coat and slowly unbuckled his belt and unzipped his pants he was already erect. "For starters I want that mouth of yours" "Diana closed her eyes and tried to clear her mind as he forced his penis down her throat and although she didn't want to like it, she sucked him until he climaxed, and he made her swallow every drop.

Amar was sitting nervous thinking about going to court. His lawyers assured him that for the right amount things would go away. As far as the scandal the media on the other hand was uncertainty. They wouldn't let up. The media would always make a mountain out of a mole hill and really that was their job to sell information to keep a story circulating to bring attention and ratings to the television and all social media networks. Amar was watching the documentary about NFL coaches and what makes a great coach the narrative could be heard over the 100-inch plasma TV. "Of all the coaches Bill Parcells his intractable style is an increasingly giveaway to an emphasis on letting players be themselves." Amar's attention shifted when he heard Diana walk by, she looked defeated and just down about something "Hey baby" Diana spoke really she didn't want to talk after not only having to sexually please and gratify her doctor but then having to proceed with the abortion was too much. Diana didn't want to but she broke down tears streamed down her face Amar hugged and tried to soothe and comfort her "What's wrong? What happen?" For the first time in a long time, she really could hear the concern in Amar's tone and the look in his eyes seemed honest. "Nothing it's just being away from my family not being in school everything" "OH come on sweetheart look I want to make it up to you, soon this will be better we go to court in a few days, and I can put these lies behind me and we can move forward, and I can get back to playing ball and get you whatever you want. Don't you want a baby now that we're married" Hearing those words made Diana confused and sick to her stomach. She got dizzy and ran to the nearest bathroom and threw up. Diana locked herself in the bathroom and cried. Amar gave up trying to convince her to come out and eventually started playing his PlayStation and talking on the phone Diana took a long hot shower and climbed into bed alone.

After leaving the courthouse reporters swarmed Amar, who was dressed in a smoked gray custom fitted Armani suit and a pair Tony llamas ostrich boots diamond studded football shape cufflink. Diana was by his side playing her part, Diana wore shades to hide her eyes, but she was dressed to kill in a white chiffon blouse by Michael Kors and a Sequin polyester Viscose skirt by IRO and Kid suede heels by Jessica Simpson 's collection "Mr. Jackson... Mr. Jackson" "Amar over here... tell us how much money you had to pay to make this go away?" It was a loaded question and Amar being young and naïve fell right into the trap instead of listening to his lawyer and just avoiding the reporters and say no comment, so all the questions Amar opens his mouth and said, "Chump change... Petty Money it was really nothing" and as a result the commissioner was furious about his comments and after several phone calls decided to suspend Amar for the season. Amar was crushed and had no one to blame but himself. As the days turned into weeks Amar was drinking more and although he didn't hit Diana, he became more verbally abusive, and Diana was using more heroin whenever she could find the time to sneak out and cop her drugs from Black. Who by the way was still obsessed with Diana. Diana unlike most of Blacks clientele had money to support her habit and therefore she could keep her appearance up and didn't have to degrade herself like a lot of women to get her fix and maintain a constant High, but best believe he tried every chance he got to persuade Diane into sleeping with him, but she didn't.

Amar was feeling down so she thought she would cheer him up and went shopping at Victoria's Secret and Bath & Body works. Diana made dinner and just went the extra mile for her husband wine, candles, and music. Amar was happy

Diana always was able to turn him on and they made passionate love that weekend. and enjoyed each other as husband and wife.

North Carolina

Lindsay was so nervous waiting during intake she had always followed the same routine but today was different everything was different "Ms. Jones this way please" "Okay" she had to walk through the metal detectors 'bleep' the detector sounded off and she almost stopped breathing "Did you empty your pockets?" the OIC (Officer In Charge) of the institution spoke "Duh" she thought taking everything out of her pockets as well as the jewelry she had totally forgot "Sorry my mind was elsewhere" Lindsay says smiling at the guard "OK Miss Jones I need you to walk through again" Lindsay felt like she was walking on eggshells she walked through this time and Breathed a sigh of relief when the metal detector didn't go off. The officers were briefed and allowed to go to their assigned areas in the units. Lindsay was happy because she was not only working on the same side as Charles but also in his cellblock. Lindsay caught herself not only wearing make-up, but she had her hair done. Lindsay was trying to look good for her...... she thought to herself and said it out loud My man. Charles was her man they had grown so close over the months, and he was the perfect listener he knew her goals and she had learned so much about him about his mother passing away at a young age and his father being killed it was so ironic how Lindsay 's father was also a victim to inner city violence. Charles was raised by his grandmother and Lindsay admired how Charles tried so hard to do the right thing he wasn't a wanna be thug or pretend gangster. Charles was just a young black man trying to make something out of his life, yet they still avoided the hardest part they both never discussed why he was locked up and Lindsay didn't have the strength of courage to ask him when he was getting out of prison. Charles avoided the question as well. Before Lindsay came into his life, he was lost in another world a world that only consisted of long days and lonely nights. Cell searches, pat downs, and hostile living conditions. In the years Charles has been incarcerated he has seen men whose eyes have lost the light and the desire to live, those who have given up. Some have lost their mind some have tried to take their own lives. Some have tried to mutilate themselves Others have tried to fight the pain away by the fighting against inmates or fighting against officers but nevertheless fighting. Some have tried to numb the pain by self-medicating, using prescription drugs and pills. Some going so far as waiting for another inmate in the medication line to spit his medication out his mouth and then sell it to another lost soul who could care less that the medicine he's taking has just been in someone else's mouth.

Some smoke or sniff drugs others will shoot cocaine or heroin any and everything to erase the pain and black out the reality of being locked up for the rest of their lives. Many prisoners take to religion some become extremist, Zealots, saying that their belief is the only way and Death to all disbelievers. Yes, prison was hard and would harden any individual. Charles was blessed to have Lindsay in his life. She was like the wings to a bird. Sun to a flower she was healthy for him, and she had compassion she was his window in the wall. For how long he didn't know? Charles tried hard not to think about that but only focus on what they had now. The present, the love she showed him.

Chapter 12

Charles was up and found himself pacing this morning because he knew this was Lindsay's shift, but he never knew exactly where she would be. In the booth or in either block, for some strange reason he had butterflies in his stomach, and he knew it when he came back from breakfast and saw Lindsay. She had her hair done and make up on. Beautiful wasn't word "God Damn Shorty" "Yo look at Ms. Jones" some inmates went ham; one guy even started singing "Misses Jones" by Billy Paul. Charles didn't like it one bit but he couldn't say anything although in his mind Lindsay was his girl she was also an officer and as soon as her supervisor thought that she was in some type of relationship with any inmate they would fire her or move her to another part of the prison, so Charles had to swallow his pride and act like he didn't hear the rude remarks. 20 minutes later Charles got up the courage to go to the desk with his ID card to get the newspaper, when he looked into her eyes, For Lindsay it was all worth it. Charles smiled the biggest cheesiest smile. His whole face lit up and he stuttered with his words but managed to say very low so no one else could hear him " You look so beautiful" Lindsay touched his fingers when retrieving his card "Thank you I did it for you" she replied Charles almost busted a gasket he saw the guys looking at him and didn't want to make Lindsay Hot, so he walked slowly back to his cell with the newspaper.

On his way out to lunch Lindsay stopped him and told him he needed to clean his cell up. Charles looks confused and thought to himself why? because he knew he always cleaned his cell and made his bed "Come here let me show you" Lindsay commanded. So Charles avoiding the stares and evil looks because of all the attention he was receiving from officer Jones he followed behind her and the way Lindsay's hips and rearend moved in her uniform pants was amazing it looked heart shaped and so soft. When Lindsay went into his cell she kept him at the door and whispered "Watch out for me" and pull the plastic device from under her shirt and placed it on his bed, At first Charles was scared, Then he was really paranoid because he thought it was a package of drugs, he didn't do drugs or deal drugs on the street and he wasn't about to start in prison no way he watched his father play that hand and lose. Charles wanted more out of life "What go look at what I bought you." Lindsay said before walking back to the desk. Charles was pacing and closed his cell door and put a blind up like he was using the bathroom. He opened the package and inside was a small Samsung cell phone "God" Charles thought it was tinny too. About the size of a domino, you figured out how to turn it on went to the window and got a signal and follow the instructions to activate his minutes and best of the phone had access to the Internet. That night Charles went to the canteen and bought a box of AA batteries and made him a battery pack to charge his phone and after lockdown he called Lindsay "Hey" "Hey silly aren't you happy now?" Lindsay said laying in the bed with a T-shirt and panties on. Charles was nervous at first but then he got comfortable "I told you I got you "Lindsay said with soul as if she knew her purpose and as the saying goes when a woman has her mind made up that's it.

So, after talking for hours Lindsay asked Charles what he would do if he was laying right next to her. Charles answered smoothly "I would kiss you softly on your forehead look you in the eyes and allow you to see how much you mean to me, I would kiss your lips softly and gently as if we were the only two people left in the world and massage your skin slowly and ease all the stress of the day away." Charles could hear her breathing change. As she adjusted now laid on her back "I would kiss your neck delicately and caress your breasts until your nipples were rock solid and sensitive, my warm tongue would circle around your nipples until you arch your back and your clitoris swells with excitement" "Yes keep going!!" Lindsay was squeezing and pulling her nipples to the sound of Charles voice her hands-free because of the Bluetooth in her ear. Lindsay was able to pull her shirt off and remove her panties. The tone of Charles voice caused her body to respond, and her vagina was moist and eager for her to rub her clitoris. "I would kiss slowly down your stomach and thighs towards your calve muscles taking my time... your toes and feet in my hand as I lightly open and close your legs as we both can hear the sound of your wetness" "Charles yes please keep going" "I would then push your legs back slowly towards your chest as a grip your thighs and circle my hot tongue over your clitoris" That was it Lindsay screamed out "OH GOD Charles yesss... I'm all yours" Lindsays whole body shook as she had her very first orgasm. Lindsay had masturbated in the past, but she could never quite get to the point where she had an orgasm her legs were shaking and everything "Lindsay" "I'm here oh I'm sorry wow I couldn't help it God" "Are you alright you feel better?" Charles asked with concerned "Yes I am" And before they knew it, it was morning.

Months past and after talking every night Lindsay and Charles are an item and practically in love with each other. Charles hasn't told anyone about the phone, but he has been using the Internet to look up case laws for him and Rich and here they are in the Law library going over law "Charles man I don't know how you did it but Yo man you the man!! that case was the other piece of the puzzle that I needed. Now I can fight the fight" Charles was happy to see his boy happy and excited about presenting new claims and information to the court. Rich was a good dude he just got railroaded and being out of his home state didn't help him any "Hey Charles" Rich said lowering his voice. "Yeah" "You know you my man, right?" Rich had that killer instinct look in his eyes "Yeah no question" "OK because you know I mind my business because in here that's what keeps you alive. All I'm saying is word on the yard is your fucking MS Jackson" "What!!" "Calm down damn man" Charles was hot and jumped up. Now that Charles was seated again and the guard went back to doing him, Rich could tell that it was either true or close to the truth. "Who told you that?" "Look Charles it's me Man snap out of it you know like I know I know aint no secrets in prison. And guys on the yard are throwing your name around., Some admire you. Others... well they are hating on you, either way you my dawg and I care about you like a brother so I'm not hating on you family, I'm just watching your back now when I lived in the block with you, I didn't peep that bullshit since I got that hallway job in O Dorm. we didn't see each other as much" Rich was right, and Charles knew it, so he came clean because Rich had always taught him the game and life behind these walls. "You know you my man Rich so I aint going to lie to you. She and I are you know?" "Say no more I understand now I don't want to judge you but are you selling that shit?" "Hell no... I mean she ain't even like, that she's a good girl" "OK then protect her, listen Don't let your right hand know what you left hand is doing in here these snakes and rats sell information to administration so watch how you move since y'all is hot you need to change up. Don't talk to her no more" "What?" Charles said confused. "Not like that I mean out in the open, now you need to act like y'all fell out because the last thing you want is for her to get moved to another unit or facility well you know!!" "Get fired" Charles knew he has seen it before. The Guard announced that the library was closing and Rich handed Charles a small metal object "Here" "What's this?" "Use this to put that phone you got up inside your Call Box but keep it is yours" Man that was rich always holding Charles down. Here it was Charles was leery to tell Rich about Lindsay, but Rich was already 10 steps ahead of the situation "Yo Rich" "Chill I already know let's not lose focus of the bigger picture getting out of prison". Richs words gave Charles the chills because Charles and rich had known each other for quite some time and Rich had killed an off-duty officer Rich fought to get off Death Row now Rich was serving two Life sentences. Rich was as Real as they come in all the years of him doing time, he never heard him complain.

Charles made sure he put the phone up inside the call box. Then key fit the perfect later that night after locking down Charles was anxious to call Lindsay. So, he got his key out and just as he was getting started to open the call box his cell door opened, and several officers rushed inside "Down Get Down get down now...." Somehow out of Instinct Charles had put the key in his mouth and clenched his jaws shut to prevent from swallowing it. The officers must have searched his cell for hours top to bottom, but they found nothing. man was Charles glad Rich had given him the key because they strip searched him and everything. Charles finally fell asleep and made it to breakfast. But when he came back two officers called Charles into his cell. and he went through the humiliating process all over again "Bend over and cough" "Again" "Man I was just searched last night" "So we're going to search anytime we get ready" Charles toned it down knowing they were trying to get him angry and upset "It's cool I know you guys have a job to do I understand" The officers left him alone and several days later Lindsay worked his unit and came to Charles Cell "What's wrong why haven't you called?" "Lindsay Stop...... Stop someone is hating on me I mean Us" Charles lowered his voice. "For now, on we need to pretend that we're not cool, OK?" Lindsay saw Charles demeanor and the look in his eyes the pleading and answered "OK" and tried her best to as he put it pretend, they weren't cool, and it was the hardest 12 hours of her life.

It's been several weeks since Charles called and Lindsay is frustrated and depressed, she knows that the way he's acting is not his fault, but it still hurts, because they were in such a good space. God she just wishes that he was free, and they didn't have to go through these changes. But Charles was right. Lindsay began to notice how often Charles was searched and also the way her coworkers often looked at her. So, she played it smart and gave Charles his space so that he wouldn't get in anymore trouble.

When Lindsay pulled into her apartment complex there was several police cars and an ambulance near her Apartment 'What now'? she thought. When Lindsay couldn't park in front of her Apartment her heart stopped. her mother Joanne was slowly trying to follow the ambulance and telling one of the EMS workers something "Oh Lord please protect my mother" The neighbors gathered around, and Lindsay parked the car. And ran too her mother's side. As her mother sat down on the curb and cried. When Lindsay reached her mother Miss Joanne looked like she saw ghost. "Mama what's wrong what's wrong?" "OH Lord Lindsay its Big Mama she... she had a heart attack" Lindsay jumped up "Where's my nana?" The pain could be heard by everyone. "Where is she?" Lindsay was hysterical everyone pointed to the ambulance. As the sirens blared Lindsay realized what was going on "Come on mama get up please we should be with her" Lindsay finally helped her mother up and got her to the car. Ms. Joanne was still in her house coat and slippers she put the seatbelt on her and found one of the officers a handsome middle-aged man officer Perkins "Please tell me where they're taking her taking my grandmother" the officer was compassionate and told

Lindsay the hospital offered his kindness and support realizing that the older woman who suffered a heart attack was her grandmother. Lindsay raced as fast as she could to the hospital and after parking helped her mother out the car. Ms. Joanne was distraught and although trying to move as fast as she could she was still moving slow. Once inside the hospital the air conditioner hit them and they saw Nurses moving around and people waiting in the emergency room "Momma let me find you a seat OK" Lindsay helped Ms. Joanne find a seat and ran to the nurses station "Yes Miss how can I help you?" "Yes, please tell me where my grandmother is her name is Mary... Mary Moore" Lindsay couldn't stop the tears from falling from her eyes she loved her Nana with all her heart "Yes one moment please" The nurse looked like she was trying to avoid making eye contact with Lindsay and then she got that tight feeling in her stomach, and she knew something wasn't right. Several minutes later a Caucasian doctor and a black security guard came out and asked for the family of Miss Mary Moore. Lindsay was pacing and heard the name and went to them. When the words hit her ears, she fell to her knees bawling Big Mama was gone, and in an instant Lindsay saw her Childhood playing in the yard moments of laughter learning how to read, Easter Sunday at church sitting next to Nana. All Lindsay heard was, there were complications and she died in the ambulance "Why didn't I ride with her"

Lindsay sobbed; the security guard held her tight. And tried to console her "I have to tell my mother" But Miss Joanne heard and was rocking back-and-forth tears staining her shirt. Others looked on and could feel the hurt and lost in the air. After viewing the body and signing papers they made it home after what seemed like the longest drive ever, And Lindsay made her mother a bath. Although Lindsay wanted to call time out and tell God please stop, it's too much she couldn't. Lindsay had to be strong and take responsibility for the family. Lindsay sat in the living room and began to figure out how to get all of Nana 's belongings, To call everyone and explain her passing and most important how to give her a proper burial and wake, So others could view her body one last time. After a few calls and hearing others in the family crying and distraught, although distant relatives, she almost broke down but had to remain strong. Lindsay came across a number on old, faded piece of paper that read aunt Joyce, she could vaguely remember Aunt Joyce as a little girl growing up. That was her mother's sister she was very distant Joanne and Joyce had fell out years ago and never dealt with one another Lindsay called. "Hello" "Hello Umm... auntie Joyce" "Who is this?" "This is your niece Lindsay" "Jonathan boy turn the TV down I'm trying to talk can't even think boy...! yes child how are you?" "Auntie Joyce I'm calling about Big Mama" Aunt Joyce gasped "What's wrong baby? put her on the phone" "I can't she's.... she's gone Aunt Joyce" "lord Jesus my Mama God ......I'm... Lord I'm on my way" That's all Joyce said before hanging up the phone. Lindsay knew that Aunt Joyce was the oldest and sometimes she thinks that her grandfather may have showed a little more attention to her Mother Joanne because she was the Baby, that's why Aunt Joyce and Joanne didn't see Eye to Eye that sibling rivalry over their father's attention and affection.

New York

The basic law degree at most American law schools is the JD (Doctor of Jurisprudence) the degree permits an individual to take the bar examination which is also a prerequisite for receiving a license to practice law. So, things with Shaniqua are official she could legally practice law and was going to return to school for one year to earn a Master of Law which is known as the L.L.M Degree. Shaniqua wasn't sure if she would continue to obtain her S.J.D specialized Degree the Doctor of Juridical Science, Shaniqua was in the office when she received a call about Lindsays Grandmother Big Mama passing, and she was now depressed as well because Big Mama was so nice and funny. Shaniqua remembered how she would cook and make jokes about one thing or another.

Shaniqua made reservations and found a flight out of LaGuardia Airport to Raleigh NC.

Shaniqua was working on several cases going to Rikers Island and visiting clients. The first time she went to the facility she felt trapped and disgusted it was loud and eerie. And now it was nothing going there several times a month made it easier so she would have to rearrange her schedule because it was no way that she was going to miss Big Mamas wake or funeral. Lindsay was her best friend they were sisters she thought about Peter and called him. "Hello" "Hello sweetheart what's wrong?" Shaniqua still was amazed how easily he could read her. "Nothing well.... it's just that I have some bad news" Shaniqua said sounding gloomy "It's all right baby you're going to make mistakes and lose certain cases it's not the end of the world there will be others" "No it's not about work" Shaniqua assured Peter. "Hold on let me find a spot to talk" Shaniqua could hear people laughing in the background, so she knew he was at the bar with his best friend and business partner Greg. "I'm sorry love now tell me exactly what's going on." Shaniqua loves how her husband paid attention to her feelings and showed her the attention she desired. Although the sex part was difficult, and Shaniqua went out and bought some toys to accommodate her in that area besides that her life was perfect. "PETER it's my best friend Lindsay... Her grandmother passed away yesterday, and I need to be with her!!" "Oh God let's go... I'll go with you let me plan" At that moment Shaniqua loved Peter even more. "Peter, I love you sweetheart look I've already booked a flight and the wake hasn't been arranged yet nor the funeral so let me fly down and you can attend the funeral, OK?" "If you insist sweetheart but please know that if there's anything I can do please don't hesitate I'm here for you OK" "I know I'm on my way to the house to pack my fight leaves shortly." "I'm on my way home I want to see you off" Peter was the perfect husband always a gentleman Lindsay even approved of him and that meant a lot to Shaniqua.

Shaniqua 's flight was quick she flew first class as usual and arrived in Raleigh called her parents and explained why she was home, but she said she would visit tomorrow she needed to be by Lindsay's side. True to her word she went straight to Lindsay 's apartment and when they met at the front door, they both cried. Lindsay tried to get in touch with Diana, but she didn't get anywhere with that, and her mother was evasive about their relationship. lately Lindsay could tell that something was wrong because Diana 's mom began to cry when talking about Diana. Lindsay didn't want to be rude, but she had to plan for the wake. Shaniqua was there every step of the way she paid for so much the casket the floral arrangements Lindsay was thankful and grateful but also felt like a child and irresponsible. Death never came at the right time and no matter how you prepared you were never really prepared. Honestly without Shaniqua Miss Joanne and Lindsay wouldn't be able to afford to bury Big Mama and that hurt. Big Mama was on disability, but her little savings was swallowed up instantly and with all the medical attention and bills for Miss Joanne's treatment money was scarce. "Lindsay don't cry" Shaniqua whispered as they say in the car "Girl you're going to make me cry and mess my make up...UP!" They laughed rather giggled. "It's just that Shaniqua I couldn't have done it without you, I can't thank you enough" Lindsay said with tears in her eyes. "Girl you're my sister this money is not more important to me than you are I love you" The wake was beautiful so many people showed up to view the body the eulogy Miss Joanne prepare was heartfelt and even her sister Joyce was there by her side. Peter was in attendance Diana was not there no one could get in touch with her, and she wasn't returning her messages. Big mama got a nice plot on her grave and they had a nice family gathering at Lindsay 's apartment no one felt like cooking, so they ordered out. Chinese food, pizza, chicken and macaroni and cheese from a soulful spot in Raleigh. Everyone was at peace although Big Mama was gone, she wouldn't be forgotten. She had touched so many people's lives and Shaniqua's parents stopped by to offer their condolences and to everyone's surprise Diana's mother came by the offer her respects.

Diane's mother pulled Shaniqua to the side and gave her an earful about Diana and how she was concerned for her safety. She cried and asked for help. "Oh, my I didn't know you two weren't talking and to be honest Miss Jacky I haven't heard from Diana since my wedding don't cry, I promise I'll try my best to get in contact with her." Shaniqua never saw Miss Jacky like this before God this was too much. Shaniqua's trying her best to keep it together, but she couldn't she had been holding her tongue for too long but enough was enough she found Lindsay and pulled her to the side "What's up?" "Holding on... that's all" "Lindsay replied Shaniqua knew it was now or never. "Look I don't want to seem like a bitch Lindsay, but you and I are sisters and I love you.... now hear me out, you know I got your back and you deserve the best and I just can't take it. Everyone is here and helped or attended the funeral except this sorry ass man, you told me is so good to you. Now where the hell is he?". "Who Charles?... Shaniqua you're out of line!! you don't even know him OK so stop!! not right now please!!". Lindsay knew Shaniqua was right and she got on the defensive. Shaniqua wasn't backing down "No how can you defend him and here you are in pain he hasn't even called fuck that Lindsay I'm not going to watch you go out like that fucking some guy who doesn't even have the decency to come to your grandmothers funeral; let alone call to see how you are doing" Shaniqua was going in and Lindsay lashed out

"To Hell with you Shaniqua what? you're so much better than me you don't know Charles and if he wasn't locked up he would be here trust me he cares about me." "Holdup think I'm better than you? Lindsay I've never been in competition with you, and he's locked up when did that happen?" Shaniqua asked with her hands on her hips and Lindsay knew Shaniqua was right and was always a friend it's just that Lindsay couldn't take the words Shaniqua spoke because honestly the truth hurt. "Oh, you can't answer me?" "He's been locked up" "Been locked up What? have you bumped your head? So now you've gotten so low that you're allowing a man in prison fuck you at work?" "That's it Bitch!!! I aint letting no one fuck me!! and who are you to judge me? You were born with a silver spoon in your mouth you don't know struggle" As the words left her mouth, she wished she could take them back. But it was too late. Shaniqua stood straight up, and a single tier fell from her eyes. "You know what? I may not know struggle, but I know how to love and be a friend and all these years I see now how you really feel. And you lied to me Lindsay lied to me by saying that I would be able to meet this man, that you know I would treat like family because of you, but you lied. How was I going to meet him in prison? I'm threw with you if we don't have to trust we don't have nothing." And with that Shaniqua cried as she found Peter kissed Miss Joanne and walked out of Lindsay's life.

Atlanta

"Yes... Yes, Big Daddy yes you know it's yours" Diana was throwing it back as the sound of skin smacking against skin was heard throughout the doctor's office. Dr. Richardson was sweating he just can't get enough of Diana. And was calling her more often, prior to the current sex session Dr. Richardson's assistant stared daggers into Diana knowing why she was there, and they both knew that there was no class and what was going on. Still Diana thought to herself 'Who is this tramp to judge me? what is she jealous?' and that was partly true; Yet in a way the assistant felt used by Dr Richardson because the office was not only being used for their affair but now here was Diana now taken away what little attention, she was receiving at the office from Dr. Richardson. and he wasn't discreet about it at all. "Thank you that was wonderful" Dr. Richardson said leaning in to kiss Diana. Diana moved her face. "I told you no kissing." It was bad enough that she was letting him have his way with her body. Diana was fed up this had to stop. "And it stops today!!! I'm serious" "listen I told you play nice, and I'll play nice" The doctor said while licking his lips. Is this pervert serious Diana thought "No today this stop's!! and if we're going to see each other and keep this up, then you're going to at least treat me like a decent woman and take me to a hotel not this"

Diana said putting her hands out waving them around the room. Dr Richardson attempted to talk but she stopped him "No more to discuss not here." "All right I'll text you and tell you where to meet me" Dr Richardson went to hug her but she walked to the side straightened her clothes and left his office with her head held high with the last bit of dignity she had.

Diana was still trying to get in touch with Lindsay to apologize for missing her grandmother's funeral. It wasn't that Lindsay was ignoring Diana it was really her schedule, all the hours she was working. So, Diana tried calling Shaniqua "Hello" "Who is this?" "Dang girl it's me, has it really been that long?" Diana asked upset. "Oh, hey Diana it's just been a long day, a really long day" "It's all right I'm sorry I haven't called since the wedding, and you know... I've just been caught up." Diana was trying to show concern but for some strange reason Shaniqua was cold and distant. "Diana that's cool but what's up with you and your mother?" "Excuse me?" "Your mother you know? The woman that gave birth to you" "What... what about her?" "She was at the funeral crying and carrying on telling me how inconsiderate your being by not calling her and she's worried about you." Shaniqua just went in yelling at Diana. "Shaniqua I'm not going there with you I called because I wanted to see how you were doing and find out about Lindsay, she hasn't been excepting my calls. I don't want to argue." Diana said defensive "Argue listen since you called to find out about Lindsay just call her!!!!" Click. Diana looked at the phone and thought. 'No, she didn't just hang up on me!' but she did, and it took all her willpower not to call back and curse Shaniqua out. Diana realized that her and Shaniqua weren't on best of terms anymore. Fine she thought, she'll get over it and Diana called Black To get some more drugs. she was running low, and she needed to relax.

Two Years Later

Lindsay continues to come to work as usual and now she's been working at the facility for a while and has become familiar with her coworkers. Lindsay's training someone today so although she is not a sergeant officers will sometimes have the duty of walking a new officer threw their duties and obligations so today, she's training a new officer. "Good morning" "Good morning you nervous?" Lindsay asked, "A little I guess" "Kool so what's your name?" "Adriana Bullhorn" "All right I'm Lindsay last name Jackson and it's a pleasure to meet you today I'm going to kind of guide you through the day help you understand the routine and what you have to do so that way you get a feel of what's going on Kool?" "Yes" "OK first obviously this is a prison and with all due respect you're a beautiful woman, some of these men act like boys and children and we have to remember that they've been locked up a long time just stand firm and carry yourself with respect and you'll get respect." Lindsay looked over Ms. bullhorn she was probably 23 years old Colgate smile shoulder length real hair and her hips were at least 48inches she was country thick and had pretty brown eyes "Safety is the most important thing your radio and your mace is your first response if you're in a serious situation, but I've only had to maze four people in 3 1/2 years and that's because they wouldn't stop fighting so basically what I'm saying is most things are not that serious. A lot of the guys just want some attention I'll talk I'm not rude as long as it's not personal. "Lindsay thought about how hypocritical she sounded telling a young girl how professional she was and what not to do, when her and Charles cross that line every day. Thinking back Charles had finally after several weeks gotten through his storm of harassment from cell searches and what have you. Eventually their situation returned to normal, if you consider being in love with a man behind bars normal. Oh, and how she loved him they still talk on the cell phone and their conversations were more intense. It's to the point now that they know one another so well they could finish each other sentences. They still have phone sex and to Lindsay the orgasms are more frequent and intense, most important is how Charles and Lindsay have built a bond that is not just based on sex because truthfully, they have never touch intimately so their relationship is built first on a mental and spiritual level. without the conventional method where people meet and have sex without really knowing one another. Lindsay has opened up to Charles in ways she didn't know was possible and he has become her soulmate.

Lindsay even found the courage to ask Charles why he was locked up. She cried for days just knowing he had a life sentence. But hearing the sincerity and his voice as he told her the whole story. Charles was driving to work at Home Depot, and he saw a guy from the neighborhood who he knew, they had grown up together. They didn't run in the same circles because the guy Justin Green had dropped out of high school. So, at the stop sign Justin kind of flagged Charles down and without really asking jumped into the passenger seat of his car. "Hey Charles, what's good?" Charles could smell the alcohol on his breath and smell the smoke in his clothes "Hey Justin what's up man? what are you doing just getting in my car?" "My Bad man look here can you just take me to the BP gas station this is for the gas" Before Charles can protest or deny him, he looked at the $10 bill and thought shoot the BP gas stations not too far and he needed gas anyway no harm done. As he drove, he glanced over at Justin he didn't consider Justin a friend anymore Justin had quit school and really let himself go with drugs and not caring about his appearance his whole attitude on life was not right. Still, he had only been harmful and self-destructive. He had never done anything to

Charles personally. Charles pulled up to the gas station parked beside the pump and went in the store with Justin he bought a pack of gum a ginger ale and a bag of chips. Charles spoke with the man behind the register Mr. Holloway. Mr. Holloway was a good man older white man genuine not a racist bone in his body. Mr. Holloway had been working in the gas station as long as he could remember he knew Justin and everyone in the neighborhood and was familiar with everyone's parents, so Charles was respectful and spoke smiled and clowned with Mr. Holloway as they always did. And Charles left the store in a good mood. heading around the car to pump gas in the tank. Charles waved at a few people he knew from church and when done sat in the car to clear his mind before work. Then his world changed. Justin startled him by jumping into the car breathing hard and sweating with a handful of money. "Man, why are you slamming my door so hard?" "Can't talk drive!!!" Justin said looking around all crazy eyes bulging out of his head "What's up man?" Charles asked concerned. "Just freaking drive man!!!" Justin was yelling. Now Charles was nervous "Why I man... look you said you wanted a ride to the store we didn't agree on nothing else what's up man?" "Fucking drive the car before I shoot you too!!!". Justin pointed the 357 magnum at Charles and Charles started shaking nervously. "OK calm down man... I'm driving just tell me where I am going?" Charles said. He looked Justin in his eyes and realized the lights were out. Justin was gone so he tried to make the best of the situation by doing what he was told. Charles pulled out the gas station and Justin lowered the gun from his head and just the thought of being shot almost made him urinate on himself. Not a mile down the road the police got right behind him and flashed the lights and sirens "Don't you pull over" Justin whispers and when Charles looked at him his lips were white, and his pupils look weird "Man I have to I have license it's cool just put the gun up." Charles said trying to defuse the situation and he pulled over. "What the fuck are you doing? I should kill you" Justin said Pointing the gun at Charles and then running out of the vehicle. The officer immediately called for back up and Justin was apprehended later found hiding in someone's yard. The officers arrested Charles as well and after being interrogated he was taken to the magistrate and was charged with first-degree murder and arm robbery with a dangerous weapon. Charles cried and tried to explain what happened, but it all fell on deaf ears because he had no idea about the law process and just that fast, he was no longer free but a number in the system fighting for his freedom.

So here Charles was sentenced to life for a murder he did not commit, Charles lost everything a promising future hoping and praying to be exonerated, fighting to win his freedom.

Chapter 13

Trapped in the bare-knuckled North Carolina Justice system and eventually Charles learned that slavery truly wasn't over they just moved it where no one can see it. In the rural country spots where the billion-dollar industry of prison system boomed. Charles can still remember Vividly the van ride from County Jail shackled and handcuffed the guards ever watchful of their precious cargo. they searched the van. Stuck mirrors under the vehicle to look for guns and bombs. Charles often and had flash backs to the time when a white detective told him in a sinister and low tone "listen up Nigga you're in a white man's town if you don't plead guilty I'll make an example of you" At the prescient the detectives grilled him for hours but wouldn't tell him why he was there at first then he found out it was for the murder & robbery of Mr. Holloway and all he could think was 'Mr. Holloway... good Mr. Holloway that would give my family, anyone's family credit until payday no... Why would I ever do a thing like that? I wouldn't even think to do something like that' "You're going to jail for the rest of your life boy" Charles asked for Lawyer over three times "What for? a lawyer can't help you" Charles court appointed attorney may have visited him three or four times in the 16 months he was in the county jail and advised him not to go to trial. and if he did it was best not to open up his mouth or get on the stand. Charles was young and naïve being locked up 24 hours a day seven days a week was already traumatic and overwhelming. The fighting and constant unknown of being locked up, also the hardship of not having any ability to fight the system accurately. Charles attorney wasn't helpful after eight months he was given another attorney because after the rule 24 hearing.

The state of North Carolina deemed the case to be considered a Capital Murder charge due to the cruel and unusual punishment. So many family members gathered on TV and in the news, to vouched for Mr. Holloways character. And his way with the people in the community. Mr. Holloway was loved and respect although God knew Charles was innocent the family of the victim didn't care. In their eyes two Black ignorant boys drove to the gas station and killed Mr. Holloway for $32.13 out of the register. That hurt Charles knowing that his life was taken for $32.13 Justin had ruined his life and future for something so petty and took Mr. Holloway's life for something so worthless. Eventually Charles and Justin were on trial with an all-white jury in the state of North Carolina. Charles is seen on camera laughing and joking with Mr. Holloway prior to leaving the store his lawyer doesn't even cross examine the prosecution claim of a forethought and premeditated murder, also one of the patrol officers say he saw that one of the culprits had a gun to the head of the driver prior to him pulling them over but the prosecutor simply claims they were arguing and disputing over the money. 'Money Charles thought $32.13' The main thing also was the footage of Justin getting into the car. Gun out no mask and demanding that Charles driveaway. Prosecution still claimed that he should have not drove away. 'And get shot like Mr. Holloway' he thought to himself. Still has Lawyer just sat there. The case lasted one day, and Charles and Justin were sentenced to life without parole.

Justin also was tried separately for robbery and convicted in one hour. Next, they were on the bus shackled and handcuffed to Central prison. The viper pit which housed the most notorious and violent criminals in North Carolina. Bloods, Crips, Mexican Mafia, Aryan brotherhood you name it, and it was housed behind those walls. Charles was thinking 'Man here I am 160 pounds soaking wet with a life sentence and I never been in a gang.' See jury packing is sort of tradition in North Carolina they put 12 white people on a jury and of course a white Judge and a white DA District Attorney and finally a white Public Pretender well Public Defender and it's like playing Russian roulette with a loaded handgun. Charles unfortunately found out the hard way. Years and years of being locked up for something he didn't do. After only one year Justin Green was raped and murdered by two men in a cell in Central Prison and now Charles was alone in this world to bear this burden. Charles cried and Lindsay broke down hearing his story. For days she couldn't eat she felt so sorry for him she had compassion for Charles, not only was he telling the truth but to know what he went through and what he was going through Lindsay wept long and hard. Her first love was a decent man respectable, honest and was trapped in prison with a life sentence. God, she thought but after a few days she was determined to love him more, not to give up. Lindsay wasn't perfect but she believed in God and knew that if God brought her this far then it was for a reason, and she was Charles angel. Charles opened up to her and shared his situation. This hurt him to; being locked up wasn't easy every day was a struggle being around hardened criminals with nothing to lose feeling like they had the world on their shoulders. Lindsay had begun to want to help in any way possible. So together they would study about the law. a lot of things came to her attention about the law she didn't know, especially after reading the 'New Jim Crow' by Michelle Alexander. Prison was modern day slavery these private corporations built in rural areas of America housing men and women who now work for wages similar of those in Third World countries, exploited and hidden from society it was sad; because to someone who doesn't know about law they assume whatever they see or hear on the news is the truth and everyone who is found guilty in a courtroom is a criminal. They don't realize that prison is a well-oiled machine and a $1 billion entity, it's about quota, checks and balances "Baby I love you and I'm so happy you opened up to me, I'm not sure how to help? but I'm not going anywhere I truly and actually love you, your personality you're being and just the beat of your heart." "Lindsay it's so easy to love you you're the most beautiful person, not just woman but person I've ever met. I thank God for putting you in my life. I was so lonely and tired Lindsay; But I went to God on my face and knees and prayed for you. I'm grateful for our friendship and I won't lose sight that one day you'll be my wife... but it's just sometimes" "Don't.... don't even entertain the thought Charles we are one. And this is our test. Every couple will have a trail to test their love and faith. I'm ready to ride with you and for you, Now let's just find a way to get you out of there."

Lindsay was happy to finally have had that conversation with Charles. Now she was going to speak to the only person she knew she could truly trust to understand her issue, her mother. And after telling her Miss Joanne smiled and spoke. "Baby I'm happy for you I knew that God put you in that place for a reason, and God works in mysterious ways. If that man respects you and honors you as the queen that you are, and his spirit is right. Then you love that man with all your heart and as if God is watching you. See I'm wise enough to know, that we don't choose who we love, or when we love. If that's what the case, then nobody would be with anybody, and everyone would be lost. God has brought you two together Why I don't know? that's not for me to judge, but I do know he has made you happy and you two are helping each other along in life, So I got your back you're grown Lindsay and I know I wasn't the best parent, but I raised you right and I'm proud of you. You could be anywhere in the world, but you sacrificed to stay close to home and help me." Miss Joanne started crying. "Don't cry mama" "No.... you deserve happiness and God will help you and that man!!! watch and see everything is for a reason."

Atlanta

Diana had everything ready and set up for Dr. Richardson. She had candles, roses, music, chocolate covered strawberries, oils and her La Perla negligee she heard him at the hotel door and opened the door. In her undergarments with her beautiful smile. "My...My. My... look at you somebody's ready to play nice today" Dr Richardson said. "Yes, I'm really starting to enjoy our love making. And today I have a surprise for you" "Is that right?" Diana put a finger to his lips and walked him to the front of the bed. Played the music real low and handed him a champagne glass of Moet.

While he sipped the cool bubbly, she unbuckled his pants and took his manhood into her mouth. Diana deep throated him and made sure it was the best head she ever gave. Dr Richardson couldn't help but moan and gripped her head. When he came, she swallowed his Nutt. "Oh God damn...I'm coming...!!". Diana undressed him and straddled his face and then eventually they ended up in the 69 position his tongue darting from her clitoris to her ass crack. Diana came several times. Diana fed him chocolate covered strawberries and massaged his back with oil, and when he was completely relaxed, she whispered "I have a surprise for you" biting and teasing his earlobe, Diana blindfolded him and Reached under the bed and found what she was looking for. A 12-inch strap on dildo. It was long, thick, and Black. Diana guided him on all fours. "What... what's this?" Dr Richardson asked moaning. He played a long and tried to hide his excitement, but when he felt the mushroom headed latex dildo Pierce his rectum, he started to get an erection. Relaxing and moaning, soon he was throwing it back, Diana knew he was gay. "Harder oh yes harder fuck me!!" Diana began to pump and pump like a real man smacking his ass. "Do you like this?" "Yes" "I can't hear you answer me!!" Diana was sweating pounding him. "Yes, Oh yes!!" Dr Richardson yelled loud enough for the whole hotel to hear. "Whose ass is this?" "Yours God it's yours" When it was over Dr. Richardson wasn't as Macho as usual, but he still was arrogant knowing that he had dirt on Diana that would keep her having to deal with him or face the consequences that her husband will find out, that she had terminated her pregnancy without even telling him. Amar would snap and she couldn't afford that. Diana had dropped out of school and Amar was an abusive husband. Yeah, he was playing football and having a great season. No, she couldn't allow anyone or anything to jeopardize her marriage. "So same time next week?" Dr. Richardson said with an evil smirk on his face. "Yes, Big Daddy whatever you like." Dr. Richardson was on cloud nine "And bring your friend I like that" he said referring to the dildo. "I will and trust I have another surprise that will blow your mind" Diana replied, "I can't wait" Dr. Richardson left out the room in the state of lustful bliss, feeling in control.

As soon as Diana closed the door she went to work. Diana had spent over $10,000 on the best state of the art photography and video equipment. She had hidden cameras everywhere and she planned to compile the footage of this last week freak fest and give Doctor Richardson a taste of his own medicine. Now she will see how Dr. Richardson would feel when his wife finds out that he was not only having an affair but taking 12 inches of big dildo up the ass. All she had to do now is call the technician who set up the equipment to put the footage together.

Raleigh NC

Suave is sentenced to life +10 years and he takes it as a badge of honor parading around telling anyone and everyone who will listen how money isn't an issue and he'll be out soon. Suave even had T-shirts printed up that read (Free Suave). After being in Raleigh County Jail for two years he was sentenced and processed in Central Prison. Once there he was loud and rambunctious "Yeah what's up bro?" "God Damn boy send me something!! I know you eating boy" He went through the medical process and tried to holler at every female who work there "Damn boo what's up?" Most of the female officers paid him no mind. To Suave he felt like he was a celebrity, and everybody should know him, He acted as if the whole world owed him something. After medical he was assigned to his Dorm. As soon as he entered the block, he saw some cats from Raleigh that he knew. Suave acted as if they were at the club meeting up instead of prison. "Damn my Nigga what's good boy?" There were hugs and handshakes and all smiles Suave soaked it all in and got the rundown of the prison. "Man, the block is straight, the police don't fuck with you. Period, there was a Nigga scoring some k2, but his dumb ass smoked so much of his own shit he bugged out and went to medical. Man!!! It's some bad bitches here boy!!! but most of them work in medical and shit the chick that's working now. Niggas try to holler but some lame in here got her nose open."

The person speaking looked towards the direction of the front of the block and so did everyone else that's when Suave saw Lindsay and Charles talking "Yo watch out I'm going up there" Suave walked to the desk and completely interrupted their conversation. "Ut... UM yo bitch what's up?" Suave said smiling ear to ear. His mouth was reckless, and Lindsay looked at Suave like he had two heads. And Charles was heated, he wanted to punch this brother in the face for disrespectfully interrupting their conversation and on another note: calling Lindsay a bitch like she was a piece of trash. Then on top of that he was confused because what type of relationship did, they have where this brother who was obviously new to the block would have the audacity to just disrespect Lindsay like that. "First of all, watch your mouth that's your first and last warning my name is Miss Jackson, I'm advising you to use it properly. Now what do you need?" Suave looked at her with a smirk on his face. "Word, I hear you Lindsay.... Oh, my bad Miss Jackson, I need some paper and envelopes and a couple request forms thank you it's been a while." Lindsay gave him what he asked for and then ignored his last comment. Charles was furious he had blood in his eyes, Lindsay could tell by his body language, that he was upset. "A Yo... My man... My man...why are you still up here?" Suave said to Charles.

Charles was caught off guard because truthfully there was no reason for him to be up there at the desk. Charles was just standing there holding a newspaper. "Leave him alone he's up here for a reason" Lindsay went into attack mode about Charles, and her voice was loud, so people heard her. "No Miss Jackson I'm good thanks for the paper." Charles realized that he was being tested and didn't want to make Lindsay hot as to draw attention to them, they already went through that. "Yeah, bye my man" Suave said to Charles mean mugging him. Suave got his belongings and walked to his cell. Suave watched Charles but didn't approach, he said to himself he would get him, and that bitch Miss Jackson with her stuck up ass.

Dr. Richardson calls Diana like clockwork and in an arrogant tone tells her to make sure she gets a room and be ready for some heavy love making. 'Love making?' she thinks to herself. This creep is a Fucking pervert and today she has his number he's in for a rude awakening. "Tony I'm tired of your shit!! you are a blackmailing two timing, good for nothing pervert I'm not meeting you anywhere!! today or for now on." Diana said in an authoritative voice. "Oh, really then bitch you can kiss your meal ticket of a husband goodbye because I'm going to personally seen him a copy of your abortion and fax the info to my friend at eyewitness channel 12 news and Show the World who Amar Jackson's wife really is." Dr. Richardson spit back at her with venom. Diana cried silently because deep down the whole situation hurt her.

Diana was already emotional about the rape and not truly knowing who the father of her child was. And having to go through with the termination it was all stressful she was going to show this piece of shit enough was enough. "I'll tell you what you son of a bitch I'm recording this conversation, so you pull that move if you want. I guess my business will be out, but I'll sue you, present this conversation as evidence and I have something that you might like to see" "What bitch I will destroy you!!, you'll be working at McDonald's in a week" Dr Richardson laughed until he saw the Snapchat clipping, what he saw made him vomit.!! There he was on all fours with a 12-inch black dildo in his rectum and him making the most gruesome faces taking the penetration, sweating, and hollering God knows what!!! "What.... what the hell, what is this?" "Oh, you don't remember last week? yes you are a pro taking dick better than me." Diana could hear the fear in his voice. "God please don't do this" Dr Richardson was beyond nervous. "Don't do what? Send a copy to your wife or place a video on YouTube?" When Diana said that he panicked. "No please I'm sorry I'm going to make this right" "I know you are!!, now here are the rules you sick son of a bitch, you're no longer My Doctor I'm never going to worry about my abortion getting out, and you're never going to come near me or my husband again." "Yes... yes of course" he interrupted her. "Shut up!! And for all the bullshit you put me threw you're going to pay me $10,000 a month for the next year, starting today in 10 minutes I will send you the info, of where you will send the first payment understand?" "Yes, please just please destroy the film!!" Dr Richardson was crying, "How does it feel now? yes now you know how it feels to be blackmailed. eight minutes be ready!!" click... Diana hung up the phone. she felt good know if she had gotten the upper hand on that creep. Now she was going to make him pay.

Central Prison

Charles was depressed and he refused to talk to Lindsay. He wasn't sure how she knew this new guy that just moved into the prison name Suave by Charles knew that this dude was trouble. For one he was loud, I mean all the way turned up. He was always volunteering information he knew everybody and everything, it has only been two weeks and he was either starting a fight or in a fight, He was always smoking and bragging wanting people to know how much money he had. The guy was a loose cannon. Charles tried his best to stay out of his way and Now Charles and Lindsay weren't talking at all. Lindsay tried to speak to be cordial, but Charles ignored her. The truth was Charles was in his feelings. Charles couldn't understand how this guy (Suave) was so familiar with Lindsay. Behind that steel door at night Charles was hurting because he felt like a coward, not being able to stand up to Suave and protect Lindsay from him and his mouth.

Suave in his mind felt like he owned and ran the prison. Suave ran all the card tables in the dorms, He doubled and tripled clicked on the phone not caring about others wanted and needing to use the phone. Whenever the facility served real good food in the chow hall. Suave would make sure everyone knew he was in there. He went to the mess hall and was very loud he would get extra servings and even leave with a snack bag. Now police would let Inmates fight as long as you wanted and as hard as you wanted, as long as you didn't use a weapon. So Suave set up fight night. So, Inmates and officers would place bets on certain fighters. Today was Lindsay's shift and it was killing Charles not to talk to Lindsay so he made up his mind that today would be the day that he would speak. But that wasn't going to happen. Suave made it his business to stay at the desk all day long, talking or rather trying to talk to Lindsay. Suave even had the nerve to announce to the whole block, that nobody was to come up to the desk while Miss Jackson's was working. "Yeah, Yawl Niggas are not going to run my baby around back-and-forth about paper and some damn envelopes!!!, Fall the fuck back, before it becomes a problem." Suave was loud and serious talking to everyone.

Lindsay told him to stop but Suave was a clown and arrogant as hell. Charles was blinded by jealousy, and he couldn't even think straight, so he just went to his cell, and spent most of his time in there.

That night Charles got his phone out and hooked up his homemade battery pack let it charge up and dialed Lindsay's number. She picked up on the first ring "Hello" "Hey" "Hey bighead why haven't you been calling me?" Lindsay said in a sweet and concerned voice. "Why? Shit you should know why? You seem content with talking to your boyfriend" Charles said spitefully, he knew that he was being mean because he was confused and hurting. "Really Charles? please Suave is the worst thing that ever happened to me!!, and baby please don't let him get to you or tear us apart!!" Lindsay was still talking calmly, trying to soothe Charles feelings because she knew at the end of the day, he was a man, and his pride was hurt. "How do you even know him? And did you sleep with him?" Charles asked sounding defeated. As if the answer was yes. "Charles please stop OK I've never lied to you about anything, and I don't plan to...... I love you and if you weren't ignoring me, I could have explained everything, already." Lindsay said getting upset "But I'm not going to sit up here and let you disrespect me Charles, I'm not because I don't deserve how you're acting and treating Me!!!" Lindsay was crying now unable to hold the tears back any longer. And

Charles broke down hearing the hurt in Lindsay's voice. "I'm sorry...... I'm so sorry.... Lindsay please!!! It's so hard not being able to protect you, to defend your honor, I'm going to kill him!!!" Charles was furious. "No baby.... focus on your goal and that's getting out of prison, he's not worth it I'll take care of him." Lindsay could tell that Charles felt defeated and she knew in her heart that it was hard for him to open up, but she loved the fact that he was able to express himself to tell her. They talked and eventually the conversation shifted.

Lindsay was cozy in her bed in her T-shirt and panties on, listening to Charles and the quiet storm classic soul and R&B playing in the background. "I wish I was there with you" Charles said. "I wish you were here too but tell me what? Would you do if you were here with me right now?" Lindsay asked in a sexy voice. "I would rub your shoulders while you lay on your stomach and massage all the stress and tension away, rub your lower back and kneed all of the worries of the world away, I would plant slow kisses to the back of your neck and spine all the way to your beautiful thick chocolate backside" "Yes that feels so good" Lindsay was picturing Charles doing the things he was saying, and as she rubs her clitoris she could feel his lips on her body. "Then what?" "I would turn you over on your back and kiss your soft lips, look you in your eyes and tell you I love you... place each one of your sexy erect nipples in my warm mouth and swirl my hot tongue around your areolas until you cum." "Yes, Charles baby please keep going" "I would then grip your strong thighs and push them slowly and gently apart and kiss your clitoris until your eyes roll to the back of your head, as my tongue circles your clitoris and finds its way around your love box" "Oh Charles I'm Cumming.... Uh my God, yes... wee ummin." "You feel better?" Charles ask as her breathing pattern changes. "Yes, oh that was good." "Anything for my baby now Sexy it is getting late please get some rest don't you have to work today?" "Yeah, you're right I do have to be at work in a couple of hours I love you, Charles." Lindsay said meaning every word from the bottom of her heart" "I love you more and I'm sorry for not trusting you; please forgive me" "I forgive you and I truly understand I'm here for you, and we will make it through this trust God will make a way" They talked for a while longer and finally with both of them not wanting to be the first to hang up the phone, they both counted to three and then hung up.

Suave was extra aggressive today he came in from the yard with his shirt off flexing his muscles. "You need to have your shirt on in the block" Lindsay said to Suave with enough attitude to scare a ghost. "What's up with you today? you have been fucking with me about everything, my pictures on the wall of my cell, what's good you miss me? You want this dick, don't you?" "Watch your mouth because I will write you up.!!"

"I don't give a fuck about no right up come on Lindsay, you know me" "No I don't and I'm warning you!!" Lindsay got loud and Charles walked by looking concerned. "Man, why you always up here when I'm at this desk?" Suave asked but Charles ignored him and kept walking. But Lindsay in her emotions yelled. "Leave him the fuck alone and get away from my desk now!" "Bitch who the fuck you think I'm talking too?" "That's it I'm writing you up" Lindsay started going through the files in the desk, she was so hot she was trying to find the correct infraction form. "Bitch please I don't give a fuck about a write up I have a Life sentence." Suave walked off and got into the shower. When Lindsay looked up Suave was standing up in the shower nude and stroking himself. His manhood was fully erect, and he was disrespecting her because she didn't want to see his penis. "Get out the shower now!!!" "Fuck You" Lindsay was fed up she found the infraction form she needed and wrote him up and turn the report into the sergeant. several days later Suave came up to Lindsey at lunch while everyone was at chow and the block was almost empty "Listen Bitch they served me that right up, that was some police snitch shit you did" Suave was saying "Boy bye next time keep your dick in your pants and stay away from my desk." "You think shit is sweet? bitch you're going to pay for that $10 infraction, and you got 10 days to bring some cigarettes or weed in here for me to push or I'm going to get your Top Popped" "You aren't going to do nothing to me, and I'm writing you up for even telling me about some shit like that." Lindsay was furious. "Well write it up Bitch because I don't fuck about no write up, have my shit!!!" Suave said and walked away from the desk. Lindsay filled out an incident report and turned it into the sergeant on duty. He just processed the infraction which was an A15 Bribery of an Officer.

That same day Lindsay had to threaten Suave again because he was in the shower with the curtain pulled back and stroking his penis, His pencil-thin dick, and looking directly at Lindsay. She had enough she wrote him up for that as well. The following week Suave was served with papers in the Sergeant's office. "Mr. Green have a seat" "What's up sergeant?... Man, I'm trying to go to the gym" Suave said like he was in a rush. "Well son that's going to have to wait I need to read you these charges and have you sign your rights." The Sgt. read the charges out loud to Suave explaining how Suave had told Lindsay she better bring him some drugs and Tobacco or else she would be hurt then that same day Suave was caught masturbating towards her. Suave just laughed like it was all a joke. "This isn't no laughing matter son these are serious allegations against you." "Oh yeah and what am I going to get if they found guilty LIFE" Suave answered sarcastically see the sergeant has seen guys like Suave come in the system with a chip on their shoulders feeling like the world owed them something and in return ended up with more time on top of the time they already had.

"Son, I see you have a life sentence." "Life plus!!" Suave corrected him. "Well either way you can make your time easier, or you can make your time hard, the choice is yours but when you make your bed, realize you have to lay in it. You can't blame no one else for your choices and decisions in life." "Yeah, I hear you now is that all?" "Yes, you can go" The sergeant immediately put in an email to the superintendent of the unit to have officer Jackson transferred to a different post. Because Suave wasn't going to beat these charges and they needed to be able to protect their officers, So Lindsay will now be put on a safer side of the facility. The sergeant saw that Treymon Green was just a troublemaker and was one of those people that had to learn the hard way. Suave was scheduled to see the DHO (Disciplinary Hearing Officer) Friday and they would find him either guilty or innocent of the charges he was accused of. When Suave got back to the block he boosted and bragged about how Ms. Jackson was the straight police. "Man, I was fucking that bitch on the street, and she come at me like this?" The guys Suave was talking to was soaking up everything he said Word for Word, in their eyes Suave was king. Suave had all the cars in Raleigh, the jewelry, the women, the money, and the drugs so if he said he was fucking officer Jackson then it had to be true. "Man, I knew that bitch was some bullshit" One of Sauvé's flunkies said trying to be down. "And you know what? that square Nigga throwing salt on my fries" Suave said. "Who?" "That lame ass Nigga right there always writing at the table, what's he writing anyway seems like a snitch to me!!!" Suave was pointing to Charles who had his back to the group and was going over his law work clueless to what they have been saying and what was going on. "Yeah, he's a clown" "A fucking lame" "You know what? I can't stand that soft ass Nigga" Everyone was agreeing with Suave although one person in particular knew that Charles was a cool dude and didn't fuck with no one, still he kept his mouth shut this was prison and he knew what side his bread was buttered on. "Yo that's my word before this week is out, I'm going to get that Nigga teach that nigga a lesson real talk" Suave was livid he couldn't believe the Lindsay really wrote him up, but he played it off to his crew like it was all good but truthfully he was embarrassed because he got played and Lindsay had never wrote anyone else up in the unit or in prison.

Atlanta

Amar was having a great season he was on his (A) game despite all the hoopla about his past indiscretions and run in with the law, he was now completely focused on his career. And he was doing the damn thing he was leading the league in rushing and had a career high of 13 touchdowns so far setting a record, the fans were ordering his jersey as fast as the company can make them. For once things at home with Diana was good really going well although Diana still was not in school or working, she took care of the home and made sure when Amar was home, he was treated like a king and wanted for nothing. His food was ready and as always, his dessert was ready. Diana even had treats for her man every once in a while, Diana would have a stripper come through and they would put on a show for Amar and as always, her husband rose for the occasion and enjoyed the attention and sexual release. Diana would still see Black and get her fix; with the money rolling in and a black card with unlimited funds at her disposal she had a hair stylist on call and a masseuse on stand bye. Diana wanted for nothing, so she pranced around Atlanta doing what she did best, spend Amar's money. Black was still pressing her for sex, but she never gave in and she was still getting monthly payments from the pervert Dr. Richardson. So, in her eye's life is good.

Central Prison

"Charles Altidore report to programs please!! Charles Altidore report to Program 's" Charles heard his name over the intercom but he was in the law library with Rich going over case laws. "Yo that's you kid?" "Yeah, I don't know why they are calling me; but Yo can you go with me, so It won't look shady." Charles knew the rules in prison going to the sergeant's office and Administrators office by yourself was a no no... because it caused other Convicts to question your status, like you were suspect a rat or a snitch period. So Charles wanted Rich to hold him down and go to the programs with him so it didn't look shady. "Kool I'll roll with you" As they navigate through the prison Rich spoke "listen I'm hearing some talk and I don't like what I'm hearing." "What's up?" Charles ask concern in his voice because in all the years he knew Rich, Rich wasn't about no games, and he had a proved time and time again that he was for Charles. "Rich you know how we do give it to me raw." "That's all I can do Charles keep it a band with you, now word is this cat Suave got a beef with you!!! about you all in his business with some chick he used to fuck around with in the streets." "Charles was livid because for one Suave was lying Lindsay never gave him the time of day, and for two how was he in his business Charles wanted to step to him and confront him on this shit. "Man, that dude isn't nothing but trouble, ever since he come on the set, he's been in everything but a casket. Rich Bro the dude is lying!! yeah, he went to school with Lindsay, and they went out one time as a group a couple of her home girls and his boys but trust the clown played himself and he's jealous because it didn't work out, so now he is spreading rumors." "Charles didn't need to go in to complete detail because he and Rich had known one another for years. Plus, Rich knew that officer Jackson was Kool, she didn't carry herself as a jump off and even her coworker's male and female had the upmost respect for her. she didn't have any kids and worked for what she wanted out of life. So, this dude Suave was bad news and obviously was salty because officer Jackson chose Charles and the dude Suave didn't like it. "Little bro you are your own man. I've watched you grow up in here you know without a doubt I got your back, but this is a place where you have to keep your cards close to your chest. You got a good thing and with all good things come a test!! so just be on point if you need me, I'm here". They shook hands Charles knew in his heart that Rich had his back and his best interest at hand. "Charles Altidore Mr. Klein would like to see you." The officer at the desk in Programs told Charles. Charles looked at rich and went into the office alone "have a seat" Mr. Klein was an older Caucasian man. From the certificates on the walls and degrees he was clearly an educated man. Charles had spoken with him maybe a year so ago in person, but they were practically strangers. "Mr. Altidore your behavior has been positive and exceptional here at Central Prison and after reviewing your record I don't see any infractions and I see your serving a life sentence. I've got good news for you." Mr. Klein stated without cracking a smile or looking away from the computer screen. The first thought that jumped into Charles head was that his sentence was overturned that would be the best news possible. "You have been recommended for a job in Medical it's a 1.00 A Day job and you can be called anytime day or night, but the job has its benefits, to most inmates it's the ideal job are you interested?" Charles was shocked a job in Medical around all those nurses was too good to be true. Shoot a year ago he would have been ecstatic but now with Lindsay in the picture and the only woman he has eyes for the job didn't seem so appealing,

Still, he needed the money a dollar day was the best in prison here North Carolina shoot some guys worked 12- or 8-hour shifts in the kitchen for only .40 a day $2.80 a week so that was a no brainer but what about Lindsay? they would move him to another unit away from Lindsay and his homeboy Rich. "Mr. Altidore are you interested sir.?" "I'm sorry yes I am interested" Charles filled out the necessary paperwork and 20 minutes later came out of the office Rich was still waiting "What's up man? you look weird." Charles had mixed emotions he wanted to be excited about the job but didn't want to hurt Rich feelings. They both were lifers and every man wanted to work in medical even if it was just to be around the women every day to have that opportunity to conversate or God willing find a companion a woman with enough compassion to feel a brother 's pain or situation. "I got a medical job" Charles said trying to sound as down as possible. but also respecting Rich because Rich wasn't slow. Having a medical job was a dream come true for most practically the only dream left for many men behind these prison walls. "Man what.... you're in the game!!! so why do you sound so down? Look bro you're my dog since day one... I know you don't think I would throw shade because you've come up.? Charles, you deserve all good things that come too you. Man shit!! you ain't even in prison for some shit you did. and on top of that you aint no snitch and you aint no waterhead. Hey man I fucks with you the long way and I want for you the same thing I want for myself. As your brother." Charles had tears in his eyes because Rich was solid all the way through. Here he was serving a life sentence and he still had enough understanding and love to support Charles on this come up.

Words couldn't express the feelings he had because In prison as also in the world at times but more so in prison, everyone was cold, and hard towards one another. Fake love, fake camaraderie, fake concern, most shit had strings attached but Rich's friendship was truly one of a kind. They embraced and Charles wiped his eyes, he didn't want Rich to see the tiers. "Now I can't whoop you in ball no more!!" They both laughed because Charles knew he was one of the best on the compound in basketball "Rich man.... thank you've been straight up with me since day one" "Yo I got ya get back fam... Now let's make moves." Charles went back to the unit and packed his things. Charles was still a little shaking because everything was happening so fast. he had been on the same unit for years so even packing was a major change, he still packed. On the same day Trevon Green aka Suave was in the sergeant's office. "Put your hands behind your back" The sergeant said to Suave loud and clear. "For what? I aint do nothing?" "Put your hands behind your back and submit to the cuffs!!!" There were two other officers in the small office along with Suave and the sergeant, so he put his hands behind his back and was cuffed up "Sarge what's this about?" Suave asked as if he was a model inmate. "You'll find out right now I'm talking to you to Segregation Housing" Which was isolation. Suave cursed and fussed all the way but he was smart enough not to get out of the line physically because the officers would have whooped his ass.

4 Months Later

"Miss Jackson as the superintendent of this facility, it is my duty and responsibility to review all situations with high-level security risk inmates. After looking over your file I see that you're an honest hard-working woman. I admire that so I also see that this job is convenient for you with you being a resident of Raleigh, so I plan to place you on Night Shift, and you will work in medical I don't want to risk your safety with being on the units. Although the threats made by inmate Treymon Green may not have any validity, we are always about safety first. Do you have any objections or concerns?" Lindsay tried to hide her smile. She and Charles had not seen each other in four months, yes, they talked over the phone but to not be able to at least see one another was beginning to take a toll on both of them. So, Lindsay was so excited "Ms. Howard thank you for your concern and I appreciate your support a transfer to the medical wing maybe just what I need." "Well, its settled. You will finish out this rotation and begin in medical on your next rotation." "Thank you" "No problem now you contact me directly if you need anything" Lindsay left the superintendent's office feeling as light as a feather. She promised herself that she wouldn't tell Charles about the move. Lindsay would just surprise him. Lindsay couldn't wait to see the smile on his face when she worked at night in his wing.

Chapter 14

Charles just finished a synopsis for his MAR (Motion for Appropriate Relief) Charles had listed all the factors and mentioned to the courts every legitimate reason for them to overturn his conviction; now all he needed was a mouthpiece a lawyer because sometimes the court system is funny like that especially with minorities a lot of people in the judicial system felt like minorities were ignorant of the law. And many are. So, when you presented your case to them and they saw their errors plain as day, instead of wanting to correct them a lot of times they just ignored your claims, or they feel like 'How can this man know the law when I went to school, and you were running around the ghetto.' So, Charles knew he needed someone professionally certified to present the case. "Charles Altidore report to work" Charles heard his name over the intercom, and he washed his face and brushed his teeth, His job was sweet and stress-free he looked at the clock it was 11 PM.

The hallways were quite as usual, and Charles had something to think about other than his case. As for Lindsay he had been trying to call her but couldn't get through to her on the phone for some strange reason and that wasn't like her. He had to just prepare for the worst and hope for the best. Charles was walking with his head down and he heard laughter around the corner. Two female guards one white and the other black discussing something obviously funny. Charles spoke "Good evening" "Good evening we need you to clean out two cells we had two inmates ship out and do the offices...Hold up Miss Jackson, Miss Jackson can you escort the janitor around to get supplies and clean up please?" Charles couldn't believe his eyes Lindsay was standing right in front of him and he was looking like a deer caught in headlights he was speechless. "Cat got your tongue?" Lindsay whispered as they walk alone to get the supplies "Miss Jackson I'm going on my break be back in 30 minutes" "All right" and the other officer was going back into the booth to monitor the cameras.

Medical units in prison are laid back unless someone is in direct need of attention and at this hour the population of inmates were on lock down in their cells. "How did you? oh my God wow!!" Charles was so excited to see Lindsay. "I got moved big head! now we can see each other like we used too." Lindsay was so happy smiling from ear to ear this was the very first time that her and Charles were actually alone and years for years literally they would have to sneak and hide and talk. and here they were together in the utility closet, and neither of them knew what happened or who made the first move but the love between the two and passion caused their bodies to become one; To melt together lips tasting, fingers grabbing, they both have waited so long for this moment, and neither could control themselves. They both forgot where they were.

Charles sucked on Lindsay 's tongue while his fingers explored her wetness "Shhhhh. Oh, Charles take me." She stroked his manhood. Charles was thick long and solid her pants were down. Charles turns Lindsay around doggy style and penetrates her gently at first and then nature took its course. Then grinded and made passionate love for 15 minutes, But to them it felt like forever and although they were in a prison mop closet to them It felt like heaven; soulmates who had traveled eons to find one another finally. As they climax Lindsay could feel his sperm racing through her womb, she felt so complete. when they disengage Charles held her tightly kissing her softly over and over, finally he saw the blood on his boxers. The sign of her virginity her innocence. And that meant so much to him. At that moment he knows that God had made Lindsay just for him "I love you" "I love you too" "Now get dressed so we don't get caught" Charles whispered they both handled their business, and no one was the wiser. That night Charles was a changed man he was deeply in love and Lindsay slept so peacefully she had given herself to the only man she has ever loved she slept thinking that life is beautiful.

"YO psycho...... Yo psycho I got another kite from the janitor that works back in I-Con (Intensive Control) you know paper route?" "Yeah bro what's up? you heard back from Suave?" "Listen man Suave says that he has two more months until he hits the Compound, and when he does, he's going to blow that dude Charles; he says Charles is a rat and he heard that Lindsay is working in Medical now with the rat ass dude!!!" "Word... that shit is suspect for Suave to get I-Con (Intensive Control) for a Bribery charge and then they move old boy Charles to another wing and give him a medical job; Yo Bro that dude is working" "Yeah...hell Yeah, he's working. You know how hard it is to get a job in Medical?" "We need to send Suave some food back there you know he's on restriction" "You're right tell me what you need!!"

For weeks Charles and Lindsay would have sex, passionate and sometimes even rough sex. One night the only officer at work was in the Control Booth Sleep while Charles gently laid Lindsay or her back and she removed one pants leg and Charles tasted her love box; Circling her clitoris for what seemed to Lindsay like hours. That night Lindsay cried. "what's wrong?" Charles asked. "I just love you so much Charles, I need you out here with me." "Don't cry baby things will work out. Please just be strong; Come on Lindsay you know I can't stand to see you like this... I'm trying baby I have all my legal work typed out, I just.... I just need a lawyer to present my case baby that's all and trust me I'll be home soon.' Charles pulled Lindsay close to comfort her. "I hope and pray all the time because I need you......Charles, we need you" Charles thought he heard wrong, but he caught on. "We?" he whispered "Yes" "Lindsay looked dead into his eyes, to search his soul and she saw her true love, her soulmate the man she would spend her life with, his compassion and concern. "Charles I'm pregnant" They both sat quietly, and Charles squeezed Lindsay and gently kissed her face her beautiful chocolate face. "God...... I'm going to be a father" "You're happy!! you want me to have it...?" "Yes, please don't kill our baby Lindsay, I love you more than I love life itself, you mean everything to me and every day that I breath I will do what I can to prove that, To you and our child." At that moment Lindsay knew she would keep her child and she would continue to believe in Charles and pray that God would release him from prison.

A month later Lindsay ended her shift and drove home tired and ready to eat something besides morning sickness she had developed an appetite and when she got home there was police cars and ambulances out front of her apartment. "Oh Lord Jesus not again please not now." When she pulled up EMS was wheeling Ms. Joanne who had a breathing apparatus tank and tubes in her nose, into the back of the ambulance. "Where are you taking my mother? please tell me what's wrong?" "Calm down miss your mother is having trouble breathing. She called 911 we responded and now we feel that it's best she has around the clock supervision until her condition changes." "We understand your concern please come to the hospital" Lindsay looked at her mother Ms. Joanne seemed strong, but her body was weak. "I'm on my way" Lindsay found room to push the fatigue she felt away and knew she had to be there for mother.

Atlanta

"Its fourth and 3rd and Atlanta got the ball on their own 30-yard line." "Look at this they're going for it!!! Will you listen to this crowd, Amar Johnson has been tremendous this year especially in these situations. He seems to always come up big." "Amar Johnson catches the ball outside the pocket a little play action....... OH MY Big hit... and he's not getting up!!! Teammates are starting to crowd around him; Oh, John, I tell you it's not looking good if you look at the replay, you'll see Amar Johnson took a straight blow too what looks like his hip." "Yeah, that was illegal no I think it was illegal a legal hit, but he definitely looks injured." "Yes, there taking him out on a stretcher God he looks to be in pain" "This just couldn't have happened at a worse time the Atlanta Falcons are having a record-breaking season 7-0 and Amar Johnson has already rushed for over 1000 yards leading the league in rushing TDs and yards man what a break; Now lets hear from the commentator Joyce Bright down on the field." "As you can see Amar Johnson running back for the falcons took an extremely devastating hit to what appears to be his right hip and quad area. I was told that he will not return to the game; technicians are doing x-rays and we will have results shortly back to you Phil."

New York

Several weeks later "Hello Johnson and Johnson law firm this is April speaking How can I help you?" "Good morning cough...... cough I'm calling to speak with Shaniqua um, Johnson yes please" "May I ask to whom I am speaking with?" "Tell her Lindsay 's mother thank you." Cough.... cough" "Miss Johnson you have an older woman online #2 says to tell you she's the mother of Lindsay." Shaniqua lowered the pen she was writing with and looked at the phone. She hadn't spoken to or heard from Lindsay in years. And Ms. Joanne was always kind to her. "Put her through" "Hello?" Miss Joanne immediately sounded sick and weighed down. "Hello Ms. Joanne, how are you?" "OH .... Shaniqua child praise God you sound so grown up and you sound good," Ms. Joanne began to cry. "Don't cry Ms. Joanne please what's wrong?" At first Shaniqua felt a sharp pain in her stomach although her and Lindsay have fell out, deep down she still loved her and wanted the best for her and didn't want any harm to befall her. At that moment she thought maybe

Lindsay had gotten hurt on the job in that prison. " I need you to come and visit me, I don't have long and I need to talk to you please grant me this one wish before I leave this earth and go home to my heavenly father." "Miss Joanne where are you? and please don't talk like that." "I'm in the hospital and I've been here for weeks now but I don't have long to live please Shaniqua I need to talk to you, come and see me before I go please do this for me." "Miss Joanne where is Lindsay? has she been with you?" When the words came out her mouth, she realized how silly of a question that was. "Of course, baby every step of the way but I need you to come and see me I beg you please!!!" "Miss Joanne tell me can't we just talk over the phone?" "No, I need to look you in your eyes and talk to you Shaniqua now I know you're grown now and have your own life to live but please again I beg you come and see me." Shaniqua felt every word Ms. Joanne spoke and agreed to visit her immediately, also after taking the hospital information from the receptionist she took the rest of the day off.

Shaniqua was concerned it had been years since she spoke to either Lindsay or Ms. Joanne, and when she sat and thought of all the memories and fun times together, she cried, wondering how she could be so cold. Then the wound she thought healed opened up, and she remembered what Lindsay said about being born with a silver spoon in her mouth. When Peter came home, he sensed her mood was ill and asked,

"Sweetheart, what's wrong?" "Peter Lindsay 's mothers in the hospital bedridden, and she called me today." "What did she say?" "She says she doesn't have much time to live!!" "Gosh, sweetheart, come here." Peter hugged and consoled Shaniqua. "She wants me to visit her at the hospital. She wants to talk to me in person." "I think you should because I know how much you love them, Lindsay and her mother; it's time, baby, don't you think?" Peter was right. She held a grudge for years, far too long. "I'll leave tomorrow, and I think I'll stay for a week so I can visit my parents as well. It's been a while." "If you need me Shaniqua trust me, you're my first priority I'm here." Peter kissed her on the forehead. Shaniqua has been so driven to build her name in a male-dominated law profession that she had cut everyone off except Peter. Peter was her focal point her rock, the nucleus of a world and he was so good to her. Caring, always there to support, attentive, sensitive to her feelings. Shaniqua didn't know what she would do without him.

The very next day Lindsay went to visit her mother and sat with her as usual before she went to work at 6 o'clock to start her shift. And they talked her mother was very weak but those eyes they had so much life in them. They cried a little remembering the good times. "Oh, Lindsay, I love you so much!! I remember when you were a baby." Ms. Joanne could see it vividly like it was yesterday "You hardly ever cried, you would wake up smiling like you were ready for the whole world, you were a happy baby. Lindsay, I want you to be happy we don't always know and understand God 's plan, in life people often put boundaries and limitations on what the creator can do. Lindsay he is capable of doing all things sometimes we believe that we have to go to a beautiful place to receive our blessing. Sweetheart many times our blessings can and will come from dark and deserted places. God is going to continue to bless you and that child." Lindsay had tears in her eyes she had not found the right time to tell her mother that she was pregnant. But her mother already knew "Mom how did you know?" "Baby, I raised you. I counted all your toes and fingers and even tried to Count the hairs on your head when you were a baby; you and I are one heart and one beat; I see your hips filling out and your cheeks and that motherly glow, you're going to be safe with him. God has given me peace!" Lindsay's Mother drifted off, so for a while, she sat watching her sleep, then kissed her and went to work.

As Lindsay was pulling out into traffic, Shaniqua pulled into the hospital. They had just missed one another. "Hello, I'm here to visit Miss Joanne Jackson, please." "And you are?" "A friend, Shaniqua Johnson, thank you." "One moment." The nurses were cordial, and Shaniqua took in her surroundings. The smell of the Hospital was distinct. "Right this way, she's expecting you." "Thank you." Shaniqua entered the room and immediately noticed how small Miss Joanne was. Shaniqua sat after hugging and kissing her. They both smiled, and Miss Joanne began to cry. "Don't cry, please... You'll make me cry." Shaniqua whispered. "Oh Lord... these tears are tears of joy. I knew you would come; God told me so, Shaniqua. You're such a beautiful person inside and out, and I want you to know that I loved you from the first time I saw you! But most of all, your spirit is beautiful. You're a loyal and honest friend. And you're my daughter 's best friend, and she needs you." Ms. Joanne paused and tried to sit up with great difficulty but managed. "Shaniqua Lindsay has fallen in love. And at my age, I'm wise enough to know we can't control who we love, just like you can't choose where you will be born or the place you will die. Now, I know you're hurt because Lindsay lied to you, but just think to yourself about her situation and the motive or intention behind her lie. You know Lindsay better than anyone. She lied to protect you and your feelings, not to deceive you and hurt you, but because she loved and appreciated you enough. Lindsay knew that she couldn't explain her situation. Give her another chance to have compassion for her. You know Lindsay is not compulsive nor promiscuous. She sacrificed her life and career for me and decided to work in that prison to be closer to home. You know this, Shaniqua, and in the midst of all that, there's a greater plan going on. Please don't miss the silver lining, don't miss the blessing, and see what God is doing. All relationships must be tested, this is your test don't lose your friend because she has found happiness, even though we may not agree with where she has found it. Don't judge we are only human, and we make mistakes but as a friend we must endure through the hard times as well as the good."

Shaniqua was in tears she knew in her heart that Ms. Joanne was right. And it has been way too long without a real reason to have cut Lindsay off completely, without looking at her side of things. "You're right Ms. Joanne I promise I'll mend things I love Lindsay." "Yes, child now I can rest!!! give me a hug please." Shaniqua hugged and kissed Ms. Joanne and sat with her. Maybe 10 or 15 minutes later the machine attached to Ms. Joanne went haywire. Shaniqua looked startled not knowing what to do. She ran looking for the nurses. When they came in, they rushed Shaniqua out of the room. Yet it was too late Ms. Joanne Jackson died peacefully in her sleep. The doctors were notified, and Lindsay received that life-changing phone call from the hospital at work. Lindsay rushed to the hospital immediately.

Lindsay had that eerie feeling although the doctor informed Lindsay that her mother had passed, somehow, she hoped that it was a mistake. That it was just a misunderstanding and if she could just get to her mother that everything would be all right, but life didn't work like that and unfortunately Ms. Joanne was gone. God had finally called her home. The first-person Lindsay saw when she arrived at the hospital was the last person she expected to see. Her friend Shaniqua they both hugged and cried there was no room for words of explanations. It had been too long, and this unfortunate moment had brought them back together again. "Lindsay I'm so sorry." "Oh, Shaniqua, I loved her so much.... she was all I had." "No.... no, you still have me I'm here!!! and you have Charles!" Lindsay pulled away and looked Shaniqua in the eyes. "Your mother told me everything and I'm going to help I'm sorry for being so selfish." "Shaniqua, I miss you every day I thought about you, you're my sister" "Shush... Don't worry I'm going to be here for you every step of the way." After viewing the body and signing paperwork. Again, Lindsay had to go through the tedious process of planning a funeral this time her mother's. Shaniqua was in her corner once again and they talked, and Lindsay even came clean about being pregnant by Charles. Shaniqua was compassionate not judge mental. Her focus now was to investigate this man's case and see what she could do to help him get out of prison if she could.

Shaniqua promised to come right back to Raleigh, but she had to fly to New York unexpectedly. She would stay a few hours grab what she needed and return back to North

Carolina. Shaniqua had money stashed away in a safety deposit box, in her bank and she was going to give Miss Joanne a proper burial like she deserves. Shaniqua didn't want to use her and Peters accounts although she was positive he wouldn't mind, she still refused she would use our own money so she Flew to New York.

Atlanta

Amar was laid up in the hospital with a full cast on his hip and leg. The Doctor said that he would never play again. All his family came to visit siblings and parents to offer support. Diana was the one there for him 24/7 trying to comfort him mentally. Amar was becoming more and more distant, refusing to eat or talk. When the doctors explained his condition and made comments about his football career being over that crushed him. "Amar baby you have to eat something or they're going to put you on an intravenous diet please Amar baby you're stronger than this." "I can't play football anymore!!!! Why...... why Diana what did I do? Why would God do this to me?" he cried, and Diana tried to console him but the only thing that seemed to ease his pain and calm his nerves was his medication, His morphine drip. Amar was doped up, and for a person who didn't use drugs, he was becoming accustomed to taking them. Amar wasn't trying to get better. He was giving up, and the whole ordeal was causing Diana to see Black, her supplier, more often. Diana's habit was also increasing, to the point now that she needed double her usual intake. Dr. Richardson was late on his payment, and things started to unravel. Diana was trying to find the strength to pull it together, but she felt she had the weight of the World on her shoulders.

New York

Shaniqua reaches LaGuardia airport and decides to surprise Peter, spend the evening with him, and go to the bank in the morning before flying back to North Carolina. Shaniqua takes an Uber to their home and takes the elevator up when she arrives. She enters the home and removes her shoes, feeling like taking a hot bath. Shaniqua immediately hears music playing and hears the apparent sounds of passionate lovemaking. Her heart begins to beat rapidly, and she thinks, "No... no... no, this can't be my husband, Peter." As she gets closer to the primary bedroom, the grunts are more vivid and clear.

The bedroom door is wide open, and Shaniqua enters. And is shocked when she sees Peter on all fours, doggy style, getting screwed by Greg, and she throws up all over the carpet.

Greg turns around "Shit Peter its Shaniqua she's back.!!!" "Oh sweetheart... sweetheart, I'm so sorry. What are you doing at home?" Shaniqua blanked out. "You no good piece of shit!!! How could you? How long? How fucking.... long Peter? and Greg get out!!! Get out!! You know what? I'm leaving!!!" "No, don't... don't go. Don't go... don't leave," Peter pleaded naked. "It's over. I want to divorce. I can't believe you.!!! You lied to me this whole time, don't touch me. Don't fucking ever touch me again." "Let her go, Peter; she knows now." Greg shot out with venom and envy in his voice. "Greg, stay out of this." "No, Greg's right. I know now how much of a slimy snake you are. Now, get out of my way. It's completely over, Peter."

Shaniqua packed some important things; her whole world was upside down now. All this time, she realized now that she was being deceived by the man she loved, the only man she loved. Shaniqua cried until it was no more tears. Peter kept calling her phone until she figured she would need to get her number changed. Shaniqua remained firm after helping Lindsay bury her mother, Miss Joanne. Shaniqua filed for divorce; she even argued with her mother about Peter. Her parents had also been blinded by Peters façade. The argument got heated when Ms. Bradford had the nerve to tell Shaniqua that people make mistakes. "Yes mother people do make mistakes, but it's not a mistake when you find your husband in your bed getting screwed or screwing another man!!!

That's not a mistake, now since you love Peter, so much you marry him" Shaniqua's father was furious, and for once Ms. Bradford was speechless. She had no idea about the details of her daughter and son-in-law 's break up, but now her motherly defense and safety button was pushed. "That lowdown son of a bitch I should...." "Save it Mom, he tricked you too now please let me do what I have to do, things are hard enough for me as it is." "She's right sweetheart" Shaniqua 's father says sternly.

Central Prison

Several Months later "Oh shit Suave man when you get out the hole" "Yesterday" "Man you look like Skeletor, look take my canteen card and get what you want my dude damn." "Good looking. But who got the pills? Or some tree or something on the yard?" Suave was chopping it up with Beast and he was trying to get high. 8 months in the hole gave Suave a chance to see that he was never getting out of prison. And he was starting to crack up, using any and everyone's medication and any drugs he could get his hands on. "Yo where's that bitch Miss Jackson at?" "Who?" "Officer Jackson short fat ass" "Oh yeah! yo she worked night shift in medical now." "Word!! good looking" Suave shook hands with Beast and strolled slow like a zombie down the hall to his dorm.

Atlanta

Amar was home from the hospital, but he had developed an opioid addiction and his problem with his hands worsened. Amar slapped Diana several times for no reason. For things like staying out to the grocery store too late or the food being too hot or too warm. Nothing was right, sometimes she found him sitting in the dark crying about his career. He even destroyed his trophy case and awards, glass was everywhere. Amar even demanded that Diana clean it up, but the worst part of their problems was finances. Amar was broke. And the bank was foreclosing on the home, and they had repossessed two of his vehicles. Amar was reckless with his funds and as a result of his civil suit for rape and the settlement he would have to file for bankruptcy. The homes he was financing for all his siblings were being audited as well. Things were going from sugar to shit really fast.

"Yo Charles what's good baby boy?" "Aint about nothing man. it's good to see you" Rich and Charles had not seen each other in a while but Charles sent word to Rich that he wanted to talk. And the funny thing is Rich needed to talk to Charles, and it was really important. "So, what's good?" "Rich man you aren't going to believe this look." Charles handed Rich an envelope postmarked legal mail from an attorney's office, Rich gave Charles a big smile and then opened and read the letter. "Dear Mr. Charles Altidore My staff and I are writing to inform you that your case has been re-opened for examination by the Superior Court of Wake County for grounds of illegal search and seizure failure to administer Miranda Rights and Ineffective Counsel. You have a court date docketed for May 22nd please send any information you feel will benefit your case to my staff and office, Sincerely Attorney Shaniqua Johnson. "Oh, shit man it's over!!! man you did it!!" "Rich had tears in his eyes he had watched over and raised Charles in prison behind these Godforsaken walls they both cried and hugged. Rich knew in his heart that he may not ever get out of prison, but Charles deserves his freedom for almost 14 years straight for a crime he didn't commit he had suffered. "Yo Rich man I don't even know this Attorney... It just came in the mail." "What? you didn't you send her your typed files?" Rich was referring to the Law documents they both had researched over the years. "Man you're going home!!! Send her those documents, that's all she needs man... Yes, God is good". They both were so happy about to turn of events that Rich forgot about the news he had for Charles, then he got serious. "Charles Damn.... and I hate to bring this up, look Suave is out of the hole and he's running around to taking everybody's drugs partying with the strippers (Homosexuals) and running his mouth about what he's going to do to you and officer Jackson." "What?" Charles was nervous he wasn't a fighter or troublemaker; This dude Suave was a loose cannon. "Look take this, you're going to need it." Rich handed Charles a shank it was 8 inches long metal and pointed like an ice pick they shook hands and hugged before departing Ways.

Atlanta

Diana couldn't take the Abuse anymore, so she decided to leave. Plus, Amar's mother was planting seeds that it was best for Amar and his family to move back under one roof. Of course, Diana thought to herself they were broke Amar miss managed his money and now Diana had to deal with the drama of his family, and she couldn't take it. Diana barely really knew any of his family anyway and didn't get along with his mother or his sisters. Everything just went downhill but the worst part was her credit cards were maxed out, and Diana didn't have a dime to her name. She had poor saving habits, basically she didn't save at all figuring that Amar would always have money to support her and her lifestyle. Now here she was staying with her supplier Black who was treating her good. He was the perfect listener and gentlemen "Diana look I have someone I want you to meet." Black introduced Diana to a lady named Vivian. Vivian was old in the face, but her body was curvaceous, after talking and drinking, Vivian pulled out a kit equipped with a needle and heroin. After fixing things up It didn't take long before Diana agreed to try to shoot her drugs up. For one Diana was Jonesing because Black would only give Diana one bag a day when Diana had developed a 20 bag a day habit. So, Diana was convinced about what Vivian said when she mentioned that shooting the drug into her veins would give her the high, she really needed. And boy was Vivian right because from that day forth Diana would never sniff another bag, she will learn how to inject her own drugs.

North Carolina

Shaniqua has relocated to Raleigh and was living single although the divorce process was not final the lawyers handling the situation had a system and needed time to decide on settlement of the estate of both Shaniqua and Peter. Shaniqua was in a good space. Her And Lindsay talked every day, Still Shaniqua did not tell Lindsay about her working on Charles case, she wanted to surprise her. But over lunch today it all came out and Lindsay was so excited. "Shaniqua you've been very busy lately." Lindsay says smiling from ear to ear. "Why you say that?" "Well, I've been talking with Charles" Lindsay couldn't help herself, and Shaniqua knew that the cat was out of the bag. "Yes, I've been busy trying to help a friend."

"Oh my…. Gosh, Shaniqua is it true does he have a chance to you know?" Lindsay began to cry she loved Charles to the core of our heart and couldn't imagine him spending the rest of his life in prison. Or not being completely in his child's life.

Lindsay was 7 months pregnant now and really showing. "Don't cry and yes he's coming home, Charles is a very smart man and he really make things easier for me and himself by first staying out of trouble, Inside prison as well as knowing the law. That man has talent." "What? he's smart right… he was always studying and reading when I saw him." Lindsay said with pride. "Yes, he's prepared is legal documents and I even went to visit the victim's wife miss Holloway, who spoke to me about Charles, and she spoke highly of him, and even gave a statement of recommendation on Charles behalf, I've sat with the DA the (District Attorney) Greg Baffle and Charles should be released when we go to court next month. So yes, I've been busy." Shaniqua said with a smile. Lindsay got up and hugged Shaniqua so tight. "Thank you oh God I'm so happy." Lindsay cried tears of joy "I'm happy for you "Shaniqua said.

Chapter 15

3 1/2 weeks later Charles came in from the yard and immediately had a weird gut feeling about something. He saw a group of guys huddled around the cell door next to his cell, cell number 10. The door was open, and he saw cleaning supplies and a mop bucket out front, so he knew someone had just moved in. And Just then Suave came out, smiling and talking to his goons. Two of the men didn't even live in his block; they were just helping him move his stuff into the block. Well, that's how it appeared to be. Charles ignored them; he was going to court tomorrow and didn't need the drama. He got his stuff ready for a shower, and he was nervous. But there was an officer in the booth, so he felt like he could take a quick shower. He was sweaty and sticky and needed to clean up. He wasn't going to sit on his bed like that.

Suave sent one of his boys to distract the officer in the booth monitoring the cameras. See, Suave had this day planned for months since the day he got out of the hole. He had been working with the administration, ratting on other inmates, and officers, offering them information and favors to build himself up to be a reliable confidential informant. It was all paying off his plan blossomed when he was allowed to move into the medical block after telling the administration that there was a major drug operation going on, which was a lie, but it worked. And now he had Charles, where he wanted him. Alone, vulnerable, and unsafe. Suave ran into the shower with a knife out, pushing Charles against the wall. Charles was slipping in the shower barefooted; Suave had on boots. Suave stabbed Charles talking to him. Suave taunted Charles, "What now, pretty boy? What now, pretty boy? I should fuck you after I kill you!" Charles fought back, but he was bleeding badly. He had been stabbed several times; his blood was everywhere.

Rich had snuck down to the medical block to holler at Charles before he went to court. Luckily, a couple of the officers saw him, so he was good as long as he made it back to his dorm before the institutional count, Rich immediately sensed something was wrong. One of the old coons, who used to box really well back in the day, gave Rich the eye to let him know something was wrong. Rich saw a man guarding the shower and rushed him. Rich hit him so hard that he knocked him out. Once he got passed him and entered into the shower. What he saw was like a horror movie. Suave stabbed Charles so hard in the back, the blade hit the shower floor going through his flesh.

Rich rushed him. and they fought and tussled. 'This ain't your beef, Rich fallback," Sauvé said; the two men began to box. Rich got cut but somehow managed to get a hold of the knife from Suave, and Rich lost it. Rich began stabbing Suave not only to protect Charles but also because Rich knew he had gone too far and would never see his freedom again, never hold his mother as a free man again, never watch his children grow as a free man again, never get married, never be able to relax in his own home again, and build a car from scratch as he dreamed, never teach his child to walk or read, never sleep in his own bed ever again. When the officers pulled Rich off of Suave, he was dead. The officers that knew Rich didn't know what happened or what provoked him to sneak to another dorm and kill another inmate, but a life had been taken. Charles was rushed to medical, and Rich taken to the hole., but it was yet another instance of black-on-black violence in the prison system."

Atlanta

"What's up boo can I help you?" "Yeah, what do you charge?" "For you...um five dollars" "Get in" Diana got into the car with the fat European man, and he drove around the block while Diana put his phallus in and out of her mouth for five dollars. Diana had been out on the street for weeks she had lost 50 pounds; she was just living to get high. After he dropped her off, she was walking and someone at first tried to hit her with a car then the driver got out and ran up on her, before Diana knew what was going on he beat her with a tier iron Over and over until Diana was unconscious. "Bitch trying to play me?" then the man spit on her like a dog and walked off with a limp.

Epilogue

Leslie gave birth to a beautiful young boy who looks just like his father Charles, but the child was named Rich. Although he doesn't know why he was named Rich, Lindsay's positive that when he's older and the time is right, his father, Charles, will tell him. For now, she just watches them play in the yard.

Shaniqua started her own law firm in Raleigh, North Carolina. She works hard and tries her best to help women in abusive relationships, as well as minorities in the prison system. Yesterday, she sat had had closer with a woman from her past, Miss Johnson, who apologized for not informing Shaniqua about her son's lifestyle. The fact was that she knew all along about Peter and Greg hurt, but Shaniqua took it in stride as water under the bridge. The divorce was final, and she was finally free.

Diana was happy to have visitors today. After six months in a coma and three years of sobriety, Diana felt good about herself. Lindsay and Shaniqua showed up to support her, and they locked pinkies as they always did. Life was worth living again.